Tales of Sea and Shore

Juliet Heslewood

Tales of Sea
and Shore

Illustrated by Karen Berry

Oxford University Press 1983

OXFORD TORONTO MELBOURNE

Oxford University Press, Walton Street, Oxford OX2 6DP

Oxford London Glasgow
New York Toronto Melbourne Auckland
Kuala Lumpur Singapore Hong Kong Tokyo
Delhi Bombay Calcutta Madras Karachi
Nairobi Dar es Salaam Cape Town

and associate companies in
Beirut Berlin Ibadan Mexico City Nicosia

Oxford is a trademark of Oxford University Press

© Juliet Heslewood 1983
First published 1983

British Library Cataloguing in Publication Data
Heslewood, Juliet
Tales of sea and shore.
I. Title
823'.914[J]   PZ7
ISBN 0–19–278105–7

Typeset by Wyvern Typesetting Limited, Bristol
Printed in Hong Kong

Contents

For Rooti

Thanks to all my family for listening,
for feeding me and for suspending disbelief.
Thanks to Carl Huter and also to Min.
Thanks to many friends. Remerciements, les
clowns de la Teulière, les chats, les chiens et
les chèvres.

'Now the great winds shoreward blow,
Now the salt tides seaward flow.'

Matthew Arnold: *The Forsaken Merman*

1

The Kobold
and the Pirate

POOR Ian was a cabin-boy. I say 'poor' because
although he had chosen this occupation for himself, longing as
he had done to spend year upon year on the high seas, never-
theless, within days of his first taste of the salt sea-air, he was
harshly and unfairly treated. The captain of his ship, Captain
Smeet, was to blame.

'What the devil is the use of my havin' a boy like you – with
your silent ways and strange, foolish notions – Boy! How
many plates and glasses do you have here?'

Captain Smeet was supervising the laying of his table.

'One of each,' said Ian, trembling further into the corner of
Smeet's large cabin.

'One plate and one glass indeed! You try my temper too
closely. One plate and one glass – and what about Klabauterman? What of his plate and glass, not to mention knives, forks
and spoons – and of the best silver too! Get out of here
you wretch or you'll have this ship sink to the bottom of the
ocean!'

Ian was confused. He had not been warned of a possible
guest that evening. It was at times like these, when he learned
his mistakes (if mistakes they were) that his fears mounted and
he saw his hands tremble and felt his heart go bump, bump,

bump. He scuttled round the deck asking the more friendly faces for advice.

'The Captain said I should lay another place – why?'

'Why?' they replied, 'why it's Klabauterman – you must make haste. Hurry! Lay the table well and make sure there is food and wine a-plenty.'

Ian busied himself and returned to the cabin where he found Captain Smeet standing before a long mirror, gazing at his face, his deep red jacket and highly polished boots. He fingered his moustache and stared at Ian through the glass, without turning round.

'You ready boy?'

'Yes, Cap'n'

'Two places laid?'

'Two places.'

Then Captain Smeet approached the table, sat down and commanded Ian to fill the glasses. Ian thought perhaps the guest was late. He took his place by the door when immediately Captain Smeet began to talk, leaning back in his chair, his wineglass raised.

'Not bad weather at all, considerin', wouldn't you say?'

Captain Smeet smiled as he sniffed the wine before tasting it. Ian looked blank and said nothing.

'I mean to say, knowin' we've not had the sight o' land for two days now and bein', as we are, well out in mid-ocean, and at this time o' year, I'd say the climate's actin' pretty generous towards us – wouldn't you say so? Don't you think?'

Ian cleared his throat, about to reply, but Captain Smeet went on.

'Of course I've a fine crew – oh yes – very fine – all so competent; able seamen, every one of 'em. It's a matter of leadership I suppose – happy with the master, happy in work. There's naturally a lot to be said for fellow feelin' – I always believe it, don't you know. And the ship sails wi' the songs o' contented sailors, right across the world it do. No doubt you've seen all of 'em, the crew that is?'

12

Ian found his voice at last: 'Of course I have Captain – I sleeps with them and works with them.'

At that Smeet rose scowling from the table, roared and screamed at Ian.

'Get out o' here you blundering, impudent rat!'

In a flash Ian was out on the deck, quivering. There he stood in dumbstruck silence. The sea breezes spun across the creaking boards as night approached. He trembled, awaiting Smeet's orders, yet afraid to return and see the rage that had so suddenly risen in the Captain's face. Never mind, he thought; from where he stood he could always call the cook if a similar incident occurred.

He waited and waited and still no guest arrived. The sky was now black with night. No moon appeared; the only light to be seen was the glow of lamps held by sailors out on watch, or from between the planks and from the crew's cabin below. Then he heard voices. They came from behind him, from the cabin he had just left. One he knew belonged to Captain Smeet; the other was unfamiliar. The sounds of plates and cutlery and the chinking of glass interrupted the conversation.

'It must be Klabauterman come in by another way,' Ian whispered to himself. Then he heard the words that were spoken.

'You mean that cabin-boy? That – that – boy, who was here not a minute ago?' Captain Smeet sounded rather ruffled.

'Exactly so,' said the other voice. 'And you must care for him, for I like his looks. I like his wild gold hair and his eyes of green – green as the kindest sea. His clothes hang all askew and feet are bare. But still he delights me. Care for him.'

The surprised voice of Smeet called for Ian to enter into his cabin. As he licked his palms and smoothed down his curls, Ian boldly walked forward only to find Captain Smeet alone at the table, the food and drink having quite disappeared. Klabauterman must have left, he thought. But the Captain ordered Ian to serve the next course. As he placed a tureen of custard near the empty place he heard a voice.

13

'Mmmm, delicious.'

In his amazement he gasped and leapt into the air. Then he felt the huge, heavy hands of Captain Smeet around his ears. He almost stumbled to the floor. The Captain was seen to hesitate, then laugh drily as he said, 'Ah dear – didn't mean it old chap, not really,' but Ian ran away in fright. Up the steps to the deck then down to the galley, Ian shot into the bouncy round stomach of the cook, crying:

'I don't know nothink any more I don't, but I knows there's somethink fishy goin' on up there!'

'Great Galapagos!' the cook replied, lifting Ian on to the long wooden table and placing him firmly between a bowl of brown-coloured soup where odd, yellowish vegetables bobbed to the surface and an oval, parsley-covered plate from where a menacing pig's head seemed to wink at him.

'Tell me all about it lad,' said the cook.

'Well,' Ian began, once he had recovered his breath, 'there's these voices and one said somethink only no one was there and the food's all gone and – '

'You mean upstairs – in the Captain's cabin?'

'Yes – and he said I was to lay another place – only – '

'Klabauterman,' the cook said, smiling broadly.

'But who is – what is – ?'

'Listen and I'll tell you.'

Ian ignored the pig's head and watched the friendly face of the cook as he told him the following tale.

' 'Tis the Kobold of the Sea, Klabauterman. He is the storm sprite and, if he chooses, he can whip up a storm in an instant. But if he's filled with food and wine he can calm the water as still as if the winds of the world had all been banished. You see – he's invisible. No one sees him, no one that is, unless they are about to die.'

Ian shuddered as the cook continued.

'He can travel on any part of the ship and you never know where he is. But he loves his supper, that's for sure. It's said he wears yellow breeches and his hair's red as the brightest sunset

14

sun. It's a lucky ship that has him on board and, luck being in the way I cook his food, he's been with us for three voyages now and still no one has seen him. God rest their souls if they do. And that's the guest upstairs: Klabauterman, the Kobold of the Sea.'

Ian could hardly wait to return to the cabin despite the awesome prospect of Captain Smeet's wrath. The cook gave him a tray of newly baked tarts to take with him and you can imagine Ian's delight as he saw first one and then another tart rise into the air, crumble a little, then return to the plate at the empty (or so it seemed) place with several bites taken out of them.

And so Ian, after several weeks at sea and much hard work to tire him, grew to feel less lonely, less frightened of the continuing knocks that Captain Smeet inflicted upon him, as he felt the invisible presence of the Kobold, lurking somewhere near. When he scrubbed the decks, climbed the masts, or when he stood long hours in the crow's nest in rain or burning heat, though his limbs ached and his heart grew heavy, still he would hear the faintest whisper somewhere close by and he knew he was not quite alone. Lying in his hammock, as the ship rocked from side to side and the snores of the crew and creaking of boards kept him awake and reminded him of the warmth and silence of home, far away, until he almost cried, all at once he heard the Kobold's chuckle and he felt happy again.

Now one day, having sailed through the deepest blue lagoons, past palm-lined coves and crystal, sparkling tides, the ship steered towards a moving mist of fog. Deep in the shrouded greyness of the air, the men could see the outline of another ship.

'Aha!' cried Captain Smeet. 'A cargo vessel to be sure and filled with the choicest treasures from the Orient. See! See! Hoist the black flag – we'll have her soon. Man the guns! Tell the men – go on, tell 'em!'

Captain Smeet yelled to his mate and neither man noticed

15

the terrified Ian as he searched high and low for Klabauterman. He called to the wind that was blowing up around him,
he called fore and aft, he called up aloft and down below
decks.

'Oh Kobold, where are you? Don't you see the black flag?'

'Aye,' came a voice and a chuckle. Klabauterman was
somewhere there, beside the Captain himself. Captain Smeet
heard his reply.

'Laugh if you like, Klabauterman,' he said, 'but we'll soon
have that ship.'

Ian's alarm grew and he almost clapped his hands about
his ears for fear of the sound of gunpowder, but he heard the
mild voice of his invisible friend.

'Not so,' the Kobold whispered as Smeet disappeared to
roar his orders through the decks. 'For that ship is the Phantom Ship, which roams from sea to sea and never rests. There
she sails, in a mist that contains her; forever fog-bound, never
home.'

Ian held his breath but was soon given his own instructions. The Kobold told him to gather a good stock of food and
wine, to loosen the ship's boat and stay close by.

Then, as the fog rose and the mist thinned, a shrill cry of
terror pierced the air as the mate stood stiff and staring.

'It's the Phantom Ship!' he shrieked.

As if to ignore the cry, Captain Smeet took charge of the
wheel, ordered the open fire and, with his wild eyes bright and
greedy for merchandise, steered the ship towards the skeletal,
dark frame of the Phantom. The guns roared, the flames leapt
across the narrowing gap of water and the ghostly vessel
moved on, undisturbed and quite intact, towards Captain
Smeet's pirate-ship.

Smeet flung his arms into the air.

'Klabauterman – you traitor!' he cried, and he ran to join
the mate on the deck. They stood, watching the pale ship move
towards them until they were seized with a new and unfamiliar terror.

16

There, sitting on the bowsprit of the Phantom Ship, they saw a little man dressed in yellow, with gaiters crossed and bright red hair. He smoked a pipe. He was smiling.

'Klabauterman – 'tis he – the Kobold of the Sea!'

'The Phantom Ship – and certain death!'

The two men held each other and pointed.

By this time, Ian had managed to gather up armfuls of food and bottles of wine and had placed them inside the small boat that he had loosened. He heard his friend's voice.

'The boat!' said the Kobold. 'Quick – be on your way!' and before he could make sense of all that was happening, Ian was rowing across the waves.

A dreadful silence hung about the air as the mist lifted, and Ian saw the pirate-ship split quite in two as the bow of the Phantom clove through it. And he watched as the sea seemed to swallow it up completely.

He rowed and he rowed with all his might (which was not much for a boy his size, but sufficient to bring him close by another sailing ship). He stood up, his bright gold hair streaming like a beacon, and he called to the men on board.

Soon he was safely seated in the comfortable cabin of a new captain (a kindly man he noted almost immediately). As he sipped hot soup and felt the warmth of a wool blanket round his arms and shins, he told the story of his first master, the beatings he had suffered and the wreck of the pirate-ship.

At last a boy knocked and entered the room. Ian peeped to see how the Captain greeted him.

'Ah that means it's time to dine. Yes please, young lad, and mind there's good food and wine.'

'Certainly Cap'n. Dinner for two is it?'

'No three,' said the Captain as he smiled at Ian, 'for Klabauterman is here.'

2

The Cormorants
of Andvaer

THERE is an island outside Andvaer which is the haunt and home of many wild birds. The sea swells and lashes its great breakers against the skerries, and whirlpools circle and coil between the bleak, dark points of jutting rocks. A man trying to land there would find his task impossible.

As proof that some have tried, there can be seen the sad remains of broken vessels that stick out from the swirling water, abandoned and quite forgotten. These alone bear witness to the helplessness and destiny of once over-eager sailors. They serve always as a warning to others not to dare to approach.

Along the wild cliff-face, perched upon a shelf of rock, sit the cormorants in a single line. They watch the water; they wait for fish.

There was a time when you could count their number; never more nor less than twelve, whilst out upon a pinnacle, where the sea-mist rose to reach it, sat another; the thirteenth cormorant. It was often visible when it flew up over the island.

There was one trading-post at Andvaer and it was usually quite empty during winter-time, the fishermen having left after the season's work, going back to other islands or to their mainland villages. But a woman and a young girl lived there.

Their work was to guard the scaffolding poles where the summer's catch of fish lay exposed to the dry air. The cormorants, keen to swoop and prey, often pecked and hacked at the drying ropes.

Although their home was remote, its location wild and unfriendly, the woman and the girl were well-known to the folk of nearby shores.

'Just the two of them,' they'd say, 'and no sign of any others. And how the young one stares so. Her eyes seem not the same, peering out between that long, black hair.'

'Why she's like the very cormorants themselves.'

'She can't have seen much more than them all her life.'

There was no doubt the young girl was ugly. But her voice was low and gentle, the tone of her words like the hushed lapping of quieter tides than those she saw around her. The young men who had chanced to meet her could never forget her and for this reason, during the colder months, they vied with each other for the opportunity of going out to the trading-post to collect the dried fish. Some gave up their prospects of other work, reducing their wages to a pittance. Others broke off happy engagements, leaving their betrothed ones angry and confused. But for them, to win the girl with the odd eyes was worth no end of sacrifice.

'There's something about her,' they said between themselves, 'despite her rough looks. Something irresistible.'

The pleas and reasoning of their own folk served only to encourage many of these men in their desire to reach the girl out at Andvaer.

The first winter, a young lad tried his luck. He was by no means poor; he owned both a house and a warehouse and he felt sure he could give her anything she might ask him for.

'If you return in the summer,' she said coyly, watching the inky water with her deep, dark eyes, 'and you give me the right gold ring with which I should be married, then something may come of your wooing me.'

The lad was delighted beyond words. He could hardly wait

for the winter and spring to pass. His friends and family thought him quite bewitched. They knew the cause of his excitement.

When the summer came he sailed to the trading-post knowing he had many fish to take away with him. He could buy her a ring as solid as the most precious in the world. He waited to hear what she would say, pleased and sure of his success.

'The ring I must have is sealed in an iron chest and lies in a wreck out yonder,' she said, pointing to the island where the wild birds flew and watched.

She looked at him, hopeful, trusting. 'And if you love me enough, you'll dare to go and find it,' she pleaded.

He turned pale. He felt his flesh go cold.

Though the day was warm and the sky cloudless and blue, he saw ahead of him a white wall of foam that beat against the rocks. He saw the cormorants poised and still, waiting in the sunshine.

'I do love you, it's true,' he said. 'But what you ask would mean my burial in those waters, not my betrothal.'

As he ended his refusal the twelve cormorants took to the air and the thirteenth rose from its tall rock, wheeled and cried across the now misting sea.

The next winter, the helmsman of a yacht came to ask the girl to be his bride. For two years he had never let her out of his thoughts and though he knew others loved her well, he was determined, after so long a time of yearning, that he would win her.

'If you return again in the summer,' she said shyly, her eyes resting on the distant, calm horizon, 'and you give me the right gold ring with which I should be married, then something may come of your wooing me.'

What did a few months matter when he had waited so long, he thought to himself. He went about his work with a lighter heart than before and his close companions remarked on his cheerfulness, knowing he was making plans to marry.

When Midsummer Day at last arrived, he wore his best clothes and sailed out to Andvaer full of happy optimism.

'The ring I must have is sealed in an iron chest and lies in a wreck out yonder,' she said, as she pointed to that same island. Then she turned to look at him, hoping to see some purpose in his face.

'And if you love me enough, you'll dare to go and find it,' she beseeched him.

He felt his hands shake. He tried to find his voice. Then he stammered:

'There's no doubt I love you, but I couldn't possibly go out there.'

He stayed with her and wept until the evening, watching the darkening sky. Then the twelve cormorants left their sunless cliff and the thirteenth flew to meet the night air, its piercing cry echoing in the silence.

The third winter the northern winds tossed many boats to certain ruin upon the rocks near Andvaer. The sea whipped up in short, brisk gales and many lives were lost there.

On the keel of a sailing-boat a young man hung for his life, suspended by chance on his loosened belt. From the mainland a rescue team went out to recover his body. They were stunned to find him still alive. Quickly they took him to the shore and in the boat-house they rolled him, they rubbed him, they slapped his damp, cold skin, yet it seemed nothing would restore him to full life. Then the young girl came in.

'This man shall be my bridegroom,' she quietly told herself.

That night she folded the still body in her arms and she sat awake breathing warm life back into his heart. By morning he was able to move and to talk.

'How strange,' he murmured. 'I thought I lay between the wings of a cormorant and I rested my head against its dark, feathery breast.'

He remained talking to the girl and when he was quite better he decided to stay at the trading-post to work. He helped the woman and the girl tend to the drying lines and they were glad of his company. And often, whether it was late in the night or early, before the first light broke out across the water, he stayed with the young girl, unable to leave her presence willingly.

So it happened that he grew to adore her as the other men before him had loved her. On the day he was due to leave, he knew he had to ask if she would marry him. She replied:

'I shall be straight with you and not give you hope where others have been hopeful then disappointed. For you have lain in my arms and I have cherished you. I'd give my life to save you from sorrow. You shall have me if you put a certain betrothal ring upon my finger. But I must warn you, if that time should come, our joy will last no longer than a day. Now I will wait, though my heart follows you and I will long for you until the summer arrives.'

The months went by and when Midsummer Day came around, the young man sailed to Andvaer in his boat, anxious to see her again.

She told him of the ring in the chest that lay in the wreck off the skerries. She waited to see what he would say, her eyes downcast.

'I was saved from a sinking boat and you gave me new life. You can cast me back upon those treacherous rocks, but I cannot live without you. If this is how I win you, I gladly submit to the sea.'

He was ready, sitting in the boat, his hands upon the oars, when she herself stepped inside and sat at the stern, facing him. The sun was high in the sky and there was a gentle swell upon the sea. Each wave rolled long and bright in smooth succession. The young man's heart lifted with the movement of the water that carried him. He could not take his eyes off the girl, who stared out towards the island. On he rowed, hardly noticing how the in-sucking breakers began to rumble, how the ground-swell rose and the smooth blue turned to dazzling foam that spewed from the menacing rocks.

The girl's face turned from joy to anguish.

'If you value your life, or any life you may lead from now on, you will turn back,' she said.

'No,' he replied firmly. 'You are dearer to me than life itself. I will do as you first said.'

It seemed that once again the young man and his boat would go under. He sat heaving at the oars, drenched in water. Then suddenly everything was still as if there had been not the slightest hint of a rough sea. The waves grew calm and the sucking pools dispersed themselves entirely. Below the level surface of the water something gleamed and danced in the sunlight dazzle of the day.

'Where you see that flashing light, there you will find the ring that lies in a chest near to a rusting anchor. Bring me the ring and put it on my finger. By doing this you will make me your bride. I shall be yours until the sun moves to the north-west.'

He dived into the sea, unafraid of what might befall him, only regretful of having to leave her for an instant. Very soon he emerged, holding the gold ring high above him in his hand. He placed the ring on her finger and kissed her.

He rowed the boat to a cleft in the nearest rock where a patch of green grass, unseen before, welcomed them in their joy. And there they stayed for hours, watching the quiet water, looking into one another's eyes.

'Ah – Midsummer Day is beautiful,' she said, 'and I am young and you are my bridegroom at last.'

Then the night began to draw near. She saw the sun dance on the ripples of the sea, and she began to cry as she kissed him once again.

'Yes, the summer day is lovely, as is the summer evening, but the dusk comes and after dusk . . . . '

He watched her as she spoke and though he held her close, he felt her shrink away from him. She sighed and then he saw her eyes turn pink and pale and her skin too seemed to fade. It was as if she was ageing, there before him, and there was

24

nothing he could do to stop her from leaving him. She grew thinner and thinner, dwindling further as he called and begged her to come back.

When the sun dropped below the line of the far horizon there lay on the grassy patch only a heap of clothing: her linen robe and well-worn sandals. Nothing else.

And over the island flew the twelve cormorants. No one knew what happened to the thirteenth, but it was never seen again.

3

The Guardian Cock

TOWARDS the north of the land, on the eastern side of Scotland, lies the town and the coast of Cromarty. Ships that sail in these waters must be warned of impending storms.

Some hundreds of years ago, a captain, unsure of how his ship would journey there, and being a good deal afraid in himself, decided to anchor his vessel within the bay, not far from the shore. It was a quiet, fine night; the air and the waves were calm.

The sailors had left the ship to enjoy the pleasures of the small town that nestled in the hills. The captain, not caring to be with his rowdy crew, remained on board and watched. He saw the firelit cottage windows wink and flicker; he heard the cattle lowing and a single bark from the throat of an unseen watch-dog. Gradually, as the darkness descended, he saw the lights disappear and the noises ceased their murmuring. But there was one solitary taper that stayed bright, glowing brilliantly. It came from a small house about two miles to the west of the town. Then it too vanished, and the night was as black as deepest velvet.

Something stirred him; a loud, hissing noise.

'What the devil . . . .'

The captain gasped as he saw, high above the cliffs, a star

falling, hurtling out of the sky. It dropped at speed and as it descended it grew bigger and brighter. His mouth fell open as he saw as clear as daylight, each crevice, each sand-bound rock, each copse of trees on the shore. The dog howled and an owl hooted. Still the star fell, down towards the hillside and the house he had just been looking at. He was about to hold his ears in fright when he heard another, less familiar, sound. It was a cock-crow; its shrill call pealed through the night. He could have sworn it came from the cottage. The falling star suddenly stopped and almost bounced backwards. But it fell again and as it did so, the cock-crow pierced the air. The star bolted higher. Again it swerved and dropped until it seemed to touch the cottage roof.

'Cock – a – croooow!'

From deep inside the small building, the captain heard the wings of the cock panic and flutter, flapping in exclamation. As its hollow cry dissolved, so did the star take to the sky and vanish quite from sight.

'Well, I'll be – Well I never did, I – '

The captain shook his head and stood there on the deck, utterly amazed.

When the sailors returned he listened with effort. He pretended to laugh as he heard them talk, though he could not put out of his mind all that he had seen.

'Oh aye, sir. A merry time and a generous landlord at the inn,' they enthused. 'And as jovial a place as you could hope to find, to forget the smell and taste of salt upon the hands.'

'Really?' asked the captain. 'Then perhaps we should stay another night. You all look very cheerful.'

The men applauded his suggestion and looked forward to more hours on dry land.

The next night they lowered the rowing boats and set off for the shore once more. They called out, 'You'll not be coming with us Cap'n?' as they saw him leaning over the ship's side, his gaze fixed ahead, his pipe smoking softly in the cool night breeze.

'No, I'll stay here. I've a mind to be alone a while.'

As before, the homesteads each burned their warming candles that, later, were snuffed out again. The captain looked up at the star-studded sky then down at the single light in that same small cottage on the hill. The dog cried and the owl called. Then the hissing noise; it came as the sky grew light.

'The star! The falling star!' the captain exclaimed as he watched it speed towards the cottage. He heard the cock crow three times until the wavering star returned to the black sky.

The next morning, the sailors, charged with new energy from their prolonged stay off the high seas, prepared to set sail. But the captain, having rounded them all up and enquiring whether they had noticed anything unusual in the sky the night before, seemed reluctant to give the order to weigh anchor. He strode about with his head down and his finger to his lips, as if deep in thought.

'I've not been ashore myself,' he said at last. 'We shall not be leaving. I should like to see the promise of this town that has made my men so cheerful. Wait for me a while, and we'll sail on the second tide.'

And so, single-handed, the captain rowed across the watery space to the village. He safely moored his boat and began to walk across the cliff tops to the cottage he had seen only at a distance.

With baited breath, he opened the creaking wooden door, peering nervously as he went. And inside was an empty hallway that led to other, similarly deserted rooms. He looked around and soon discovered a locked door that he pushed with his shoulder with all his might. And when it sprung open, he saw before him a very ordinary looking cockerel. It strutted up and down across the bare, dusty floor. Quickly, and without hesitation, the captain gathered the bird beneath his arm.

'This creature can protect a lonely house. Think what it might do for my ship and for me,' he said to himself.

He carried his treasure back to his own cabin and gave the command to sail.

28

Unknown to the sailors, the cock accompanied them on all their daunting voyages. When the skies and the seas threatened danger, the great vessel bounded forward relentlessly. Though the men often cried in alarm, their captain smiled and told them to fear not. And the cock, though saving them from many a near disaster in those wild, northern waters, was never discovered. No, they didn't think to look for such a thing, for it never made a sound. It was as though it had lost its voice.

One day, having sailed past the rocky promontories of the west, beyond Islay and Jura, round the head of the land, heading south of the Shetlands, the captain, studying his map, spied the name of Cromarty.

'I shall cast anchor at that spot again,' he said to himself.

The ship arrived in daylight and though no lights marked the several locations of the houses, the captain knew at once that something had changed. He strained his eyes and furrowed his brow. He squinted hard, but try as he might, no cottage on the hilltop could he see. At the first opportunity, he rowed across to the village and walked to the top of that same hill. And there, gaping and black and dark as the deepest cavern, he found a huge, smouldering hole where the house once had been.

He ran back down to the inn.

'What has happened? What was it caused that strange phenomenon?' he asked the innkeeper.

'Ah,' came the reply. 'Ah well, that was not long after you sailed afore, the very night you and your men left the bay it was. A bright light, a meteor, fell from Heaven and crashed into the earth, taking with it that sturdy little house that stood within its path. 'Tis lucky no man lived there, but strangely, since that time, we've not been able to sleep for fear of what the unknown elements may have in store for us.'

The captain left the inn in silence. He did not return to his row-boat at once. For long hours, until the sun began to set, he sat upon the hillside, looking out towards his ship. As it rocked in the bay, with the straight line of the horizon behind it, he thought how he, in charge of all his men, had need of greater courage, greater strength and faith to see them on their travels. And here, deprived of their guardian cock, the villagers were left as the sailors would be, if ever he were to lose heart, or worse, abandon them.

Three weeks the ship remained in the bay and during that time, on fresh, fine turf, a cottage was built upon the hill above the town. Though they could not say why, the villagers found they were oddly glad, happy and reassured.

No one had seen the dark figure of a man creep stealthily towards the higher ground and into the new front door of the house. No one knew that beneath his arms he carried a bundle that moved and twitched, nor that the same figure had left empty handed.

But they watched the ship as it circled and turned, as the tide swelled and the winds gathered. They watched as it left the bay and went out to meet the open sea.

4

Why the Sea is Salt

THERE were once two brothers; one was very rich and one very poor. They didn't like each other much. Every Christmas Eve, as he saw the preparations for feasting and celebrations being made, the poor brother grew saddened, remembering the meagre scraps he and his wife had in their kitchen.

'Could you not spare a bit of bacon for us this year?' he asked his wealthy brother.

'How tiresome you are!' came the reply. 'But you shall have what you desire on one condition.'

'What's that?'

'Say "yes" to me first.'

'Yes. I will do as you say if you give me some food.'

'Very well,' said the rich brother, hurling a large leg of ham across the room. 'Now leave my presence and leave my house. Go far away into the depths of the wood and into the Hall that stands there; Dead Man's Hall.'

Thrilled by the sight of the ham, which he recovered from the floor immediately, the poor brother agreed to go at once. Besides, he was not one to break a promise.

He set out towards the wood in good cheer, gazing up at the bright, star-filled sky, whistling as he went. But as the branches of the woodland trees loomed up beside him and stretched overhead, across a dimly lit path, he grew cold and afraid. After some hours, when he had jumped at the sounds of the night and the darkness, an owl hooting, a sudden scurry in the leaves at his feet, he was momentarily glad to see the shape and form of a large house ahead of him. Approaching nearer, he saw ghostly, coiling tendrils that swathed each wall and the sloping roof. The windows, between the branches, were lit by a pale, grey light. He almost turned to run away, when a voice from the trees made him stop.

'You must take care if you go in there.'

He looked round and saw a very bent, very old man whose long, white beard trailed the ferny floor of the wood.

'They will want to buy that ham from you,' the old man went on. 'The people there, if people you can call them, they buy and sell and think not of the body's needs, nor the growth of the soul. They will see that you carry something, and the greed in their hearts will make them yearn for it. You must be careful.'

'Then what shall I do? Shall I leave the moment I have entered?'

'That will be difficult. Go and watch and listen. And if they insist on taking your food, then ask for something in return.'

'But what? This ham is food for my wife and myself. This food is what we most need.'

'Ask for the handmill that stands behind the door.'

The poor man stared again at the large, dark house and remembered his promise to his brother.

'Go on then,' the old man urged. 'And when you have the handmill, come back to me. I will teach you its secret that few people know.'

Confused, but strangely intrigued, the poor man went forward and stepped inside the door of Dead Man's Hall.

Sure enough, their eyes widened and glistened. The creatures, whose heads sprouted little horns, whose jackets flapped above forked tails, turned and faced him instantly.

They saw the ham and shouted and begged him to give it up.

'This is my Christmas dinner. I cannot let you have it,' he exclaimed, hoping he sounded bold.

'Oh but you must – we must have it. Give it to us,' they pleaded, as their hands grappled the air towards him.

'Only if I can have the handmill that stands behind the door,' he announced.

They scurried and hurried and complained, but at last they wrenched the ham from his grasp and left him standing alone, their interest in him having vanished completely.

Quickly he reached for the handmill and ran from the door. He went on running until the old man in the wood called to him.

'Hallo there – the secret. The great secret of the handmill – have you forgotten?"

'What is it?' asked the poor man. In his haste he had, indeed, almost forgotten what the old man had said to him.

'The secret of the handmill is to know how to stop it.'

'To stop it?'

'Yes. Come. Stay here a while and I will rehearse you. It is but a simple command.'

At length they parted company and the poor man made his way home, glad to be leaving the wood and the horrible creatures of Dead Man's Hall, yet a little unsure of the prize he had gained.

Wondering what had kept him so long, his wife welcomed him eagerly.

'Has your brother spared a thought for us this year?' she asked.

The poor man recovered his breath and, trying to look calm, placed the little wooden handmill on the table.

'I have this handmill,' he said.

'Handmill? And what shall we do with a handmill?' said his exasperated wife. 'Shall we eat it? Shall we milk it? What use is this when we are nearly starving?'

He felt ashamed. He remembered passing by his brother's

house on his way home and all that he had seen there; the warm firelight, the gaily coloured decorations, above all, the tables laden with delicious food.

'Oh, how I wish we had a table spread like that, with meat and fruit and wine a-plenty,' he sighed.

A loud creak resounded from the handmill. Its handle turned, slowly at first, but then in rhythmic motion. And as it moved, so they watched whole joints of beef and fowl, a turkey (neatly stuffed and surrounded by crisp, brown sausages), potatoes boiled, mashed and roasted, vegetables, sauces and pastries galore, each squeezing from the handmill together with its own perfectly sized dish. Then came the pinkest of blancmanges, the richest of fruit puddings decked with a sprig of holly, and all ablaze in brandy.

At last the poor man leaned forward and whispered the words he had been taught.

'Grind slowly now, then slow till you stop.'

The couple hugged each other with happiness.

'Oh, let us share this feast with our friends,' they declared, and within the hour their parlour was bustling with the joyful sounds of merry-making.

The news of this Christmas blessing spread fast round the neighbourhood until it reached the house of the wealthy brother of the poor man. Confounded by what he heard, he stormed from his own celebrations and marched to the other end of the village. As he opened his brother's door he cursed and swore.

' . . . and what the Devil has brought this about?'

'What the Devil indeed. Why do you need to know?' said the poor man, smiling to himself.

'Because I must know. How has this feast come about?'

'I have to thank my handmill for it. See, there, upon the table. I need only ask it to grind me anything I wish and it will obey me.'

'Then I must have this handmill. What shall I give you for it?'

'It is beyond price.'

'But I must have it. Give it to me, I say!'

The rich brother stamped as he insisted. His face grew red with rage and tears filled his eyes. He was making such an exhibition of himself, that the poor man, feeling a measure of sympathy for him, at last agreed to part with the handmill.

'If it means so very much to you, then take it. Wait until harvest though. Then I know I shall have enough food for the coming winter.'

The rich man left satisfied.

In the days that followed the poor man and his wife shared many splendid meals with neighbours and friends who, like them, would otherwise have gone to bed hungry each night. In the spring the handmill continued to provide, but it was not only food that was asked of it. Sometimes, when the evenings had still not reached their summer length, and the poor man felt he could work a few hours longer, he asked the mill for light. Always his requests were granted. By August, the poor man knew he would soon have to give up his treasured handmill, but he was not grieved; he was grateful for all that the mill had given him. He was not afraid of being poor again.

The day came when the rich brother arrived at his cottage door to claim the mill and no sooner did he have it in his possession than he sped home, placed it on his long, oak table and commanded it to work.

'Herrings. I want herrings tonight. Herrings and creamy soup.'

Now it so happened that the rich man's wife, despite their wealth, liked to help in the fields at harvest time. When she had left their home that morning she had been anxious about what to make for their supper. Being out all day she would not have the time to prepare anything special.

'Leave it to me,' her husband had said, and though she protested he was no good in the kitchen, she was pleased at his thoughtfulness. During the day she wondered what treat he would have in store for her and as she waved goodbye to the other women, she turned to make her way back to their home with a smile on her face and a lightness in her heart.

She climbed the fence and stared up at the golden light in the sky and sighed with pleasure, knowing she would not have to busy herself further that evening. Then she stood still. At the bottom of the corn-filled valley she saw something that made her feel peculiarly uneasy.

The river had disappeared and in its place was a wide lake of a strange, yellowy substance. She sniffed the air and thought that perhaps the sea had flooded, so strong was the smell of fish. On venturing closer, she saw the lake was rising at an alarming pace, filling not with water, but with milk pottage and herrings. She strained her eyes to see what had caused this phenomenon and to her alarm, she discovered that the source of the unnatural flow was her very own house. The soup and fish spewed from every window.

She ran to the bridge and was able to cross it before it too had become engulfed by the fishy flood. She saw her husband, stranded on the highest chimney of their roof. He was calling to her.

'Go and fetch my brother – bring him here! Tell him he can have the mill, but bring him here as fast as your legs will take you.'

When he heard the news, the poor man understood what had happened and he arrived at his brother's house just as the soup had reached the level of the ground floor window-sills. He climbed the vines to the upper storey and disappeared indoors to find the handmill.

'Grind slowly now, then slow till you stop,' he said, as his brother continued to bellow and bawl from the chimney-tops.

Soon, the torrent ceased and the lake dispersed, leaving countless herrings dotted about the valley in a creamy swamp.

On arriving home again, the poor man summoned his wife

to his side and together they stared at the handmill as it stood where it previously had been, in the centre of the kitchen table.

'I've been thinking,' he said, 'and I've decided it's best to leave this place. My handmill has caused so much trouble, as well as joy. My brother is impossible and he will torment me to know the secret of the mill's control. We have become too famous.'

'Where shall we go?' asked his wife.

'Wherever we want. With the mill we can build a house to our own requirements. Where would you like to live?'

'I should like to live near the sea.'

It was not long before they packed up their favourite belongings, leaving their small cottage to friends whose needs were few and simple. With the handmill securely tucked beneath his arm, the poor man and his wife arrived at the edge of the land from where they could see, on one side, the wide, rolling fields and on the other, the vast blue space of the open sea.

'This is the perfect spot,' they declared.

The afternoon sun was bright and warm when they set the mill on the ground.

'Now build us a farmhouse; a house whose walls are as golden as the leaves of this lovely autumn season.'

And so the mill began to grind. They stood back as they watched each piece of timber squeeze from the small, rolling wheels. Then nails, each one made of pure gold, that flew up and banged the beams and floors, the windows and doors, into place. At last the farmhouse was almost complete.

'Grind slowly now, then slow till you stop,' called the poor man, and when the last tile had been edged into place upon the golden roof and the sun was almost set across the sea, he saw how the walls of the house shone brightly on to the water, lending the crests of the waves a brilliant glow.

Content with all that they owned the poor man and his wife required of the handmill only food when their provisions ran low. They soon discovered, however, that the fame they were

38

eager to lose was becoming unavoidable. Tales of the golden farmhouse reached beyond their immediate vicinity. Beyond the shores of their country, even to the far corners of the world, people grew to hear about the house that gleamed from the cliffs. Mariners altered course to find that part of the coast where they might catch a glimpse of the wonderful sight. Often, when they thought they were quite alone with no travellers to disturb them, the poor man and his wife would hear the sound of cannons firing, or the roar of a ship's horn outside their windows. Then they'd look and see what amounted to almost a fleet of varied ships and boats, all spread across the bay, basking in the light of the golden walls' rays.

It happened that one day, a skipper who had heard of the handmill and all it had brought the couple, moored his freighter in the bay and was soon scrambling up the cliff path to meet these fortunate owners. He muttered as he went:

'Why, if I were to possess such a thing I'd never have the need to work again. I'm tired of roaming the seas. I hate the smells and I hate the sounds. I hate the sight of the empty blue and the company of sailing men. I want to be grand myself. If I could get this mill to do my work, I'd make a profit speedily. Then I could sit back and watch 'em at it.'

He was greeted by the poor man and his wife. Though they tired of frequent visitors, they never forgot the days when they had little to own but good friends.

'See here,' said the skipper, 'I've been a trading man all my adult days and some when, as a lad, I was put out to sea. Not much flesh on my bones then, and not so much now . . . .'

He held out his bare, brown arms to show the couple. They saw the red bumps and livid cuts in the flesh that told of the hardship of his profession. They felt very sorry for the skipper.

'And after a time it gets hard on the eyes, all that blue. Just a line across the end o' the sky that'll drive your brain crazy for other sights.'

'Dear oh dear,' said the poor man's wife, decidedly anxious

by now. The skipper saw his words were creating an impression on the pair.

'And I'm getting on. 'Tis a long way I go, to the other side o' the world. Salt it is I buy there, and I brings it back here to sell. But my crew is hard to manage, now when my senses grow dim. Why – sometimes I'm afeard of mutiny.'

The poor man and his wife were aghast. They'd heard tales of rebel crews and captains forced against their wills. This man was surely to be helped.

'So you see,' said the skipper, as he spied the handmill on the table, a glint in his eye winking as he guessed at the luck that would soon come his way, 'if I was to have something – well, something that might ease the burden of my parting years, then I might die in peace.'

The couple moved to the end of the parlour and whispered together as the skipper tried to stifle the pleasure he felt at the speed of his success. As they approached him, he stood upright and furrowed his brows to form a melancholy expression, one that he knew would touch them to their hearts.

'We have decided that you may have our handmill,' they announced, and before the poor man could explain how to use it, the skipper had gone, leaving on the table, in place of the handmill, a few golden coins.

They watched him race across the cliffs.

'Let's hope no harm will come of it . . . .' said the poor man.

'Let's be thankful with all that we own,' said his wife.

Down on the shore, the skipper leapt into his row-boat and laughed as he splashed and heaved the oars with his rough, bare arms. On reaching the freighter, he bellowed his commands to a sulking, pale-faced boy who had watched him clamber from the cliff-top and dreaded his arrival back.

'We shall be rich, you fool. Rich and grand beyond our wildest dreams. There'll be no more crossin' the Southern Seas for us my lad. Now get this boat far from the coast where no man may find us.'

The boat sailed away, out of sight of land on every side. The skipper summoned his disbelieving, weary crew to the deck. He made them stand in a circle round the handmill.

'From now on, you snivelling fools, our luck is in. There'll be no more work for any of us. This contraption here will provide as much salt, and more, as would keep us trading for years and years. So now . . . .'

He squatted on the floor and stared at the little wooden handmill.

'Grind salt. Grind salt and grind it quickly and well.'

To the amazement and delight of the skipper and the crew, the mill began to roll. From it came salt, pouring like water.

'Ha ha, it works!' the skipper cried and the listless crew managed to find it in their bones to dance an eightsome reel together, in celebration.

On and on the handmill ground. On until the decks were covered with a carpet of white salt that fell like waterfalls into the hold and between the tiniest crack of every plank until the water level rose about the sides of the ship.

On and on it ground. And when the dancing stopped, the skipper was heard to shout once more, this time with fear.

'Stop! Stop I say. Stop you wretched handmill. Enough is enough.'

The handmill went on grinding salt.

'Quick men – let's turn and sail to land. Quick, back to the coast where the golden farmhouse glows. Back I say . . . .'

They turned the small ship round, but the weight of the salt dragged it down. The skipper and his crew screamed to the winds and no one heard as their ship steadily sank.

And there, wherever it is, the handmill obeys its final command. The poor man, unable to trace it again, could not give the order to stop. It lies at the bottom of the sea, spouting salt for ever.

5

The Black Dragon
of the
Sea of Dunting

MEN of learning, men who have delved deep into the dustiest archives and those whose brains are stuffed with obscure information: sometimes the simple truth will pass by their eyes unnoticed, as they seek to answer 'how?' and 'why?' with a call for proof.

I will tell you a tale of wonder and disbelief, though you may believe it if you like.

There was once a Chinese fisherman who used to take his boat not far from the shores of his home, but who, one day, without really thinking much about it, travelled to a distant region of the sea, one he had not approached before. He stopped and looked around. It didn't seem so very different from his own normal fishing ground. In the distance he saw the purple mountains rise into the majestic peaks of snow-capped volcanoes. The water was calm and clear. He peeped over the edge of his boat.

'That's odd,' he said to himself, for he swore he could see another hill, a brilliant green hill, there beneath the surface of the sea. He leaned forward to study it more closely.

'That's even odder,' he mused. He saw that at the summit of the green hill there was a large, dark hole. He squinted, then rubbed his eyes.

It was when he moved just that little bit further, with his nose practically touching the water, that he slipped and fell. He fell and he fell and he dropped right through that strange, gaping hole.

When he landed (and I may add it was with a considerable bump, despite the support of the water on the way down) he found himself surrounded by a forest of pine trees. They stretched from where he sat in long, straight avenues. It seemed to him he was at the centre of a thousand circles. Ferns rose and blew gently round the slender trunks of the trees. The floor of the forest, not surprisingly, was of sand; soft, golden sand that fell from his slippers in tiny cascades. At last he decided he should go somewhere. But where?

He started off in one direction and after a little while he saw something gleam at the end of the circling pines. On moving closer (he began to tiptoe by now; he could tell he was in a mysterious kingdom – it had that special feel about it) he found he was confronted by a vast, dark palace. No wonder he hadn't been able to see it before; its walls were of deepest jade and as far as he could see, these walls lined the forest itself. He realized that the green hill was the centre of the kingdom; the hole its only entrance.

He stared, unsure of what to do next. Then he heard a creaking noise. It came from the walls. Before he could think further, a huge door was opened before him and inside were corridors of precious stone and gems and more doors, many of them, that reached as high as the pines, that seemed to go on for ever. He walked ahead.

'Since I'm here, I may as well see what there is to see,' he told himself.

Down the lofty halls of stone, through the giant doors he went until he reached an open space (it wasn't open actually, but its roof was so high above him, he couldn't even see it). There were arches and pillars of jade, each encrusted with smooth sparkling jewels. It was enough just to stare at this grandeur, but the fisherman's eye turned to the centre of the space where, on the pale, marble floor he saw a large, black dragon fast asleep.

'Now what shall I do?' he thought.

Luckily the dragon remained very still. As he watched it, and each jet-coloured, crusty scale of its body, he saw that it lay coiled round a pearl; and the pearl was very big, the size of an orange.

'Oh I say, what I'd give to be able to take that pearl and present it to the Emperor,' he thought immediately. 'He could keep it in his museum and perhaps, being glad of it, might reward me sufficiently to keep my family well fed for years.'

As he imagined a future of less hardship, he was tempted to try his luck. He crept carefully towards the dragon. Then, almost at the same time, he noticed the dragon's nose begin to twitch. The dragon raised its huge head. It yawned and grimaced then it opened wide its tremendous mouth and sneezed. The fisherman stood still, watching. Not once, but twice, and so many times, did the dragon sneeze, that the fisherman no longer counted. Instead, he ran forward and laid his hands on the huge pearl.

The dragon by now was completely overcome by sneezing. It threw its head about, half-closing its eyes, and it lifted a great claw before it as if to keep the fisherman as far away as possible.

Without bothering to stay and see what would happen, the fisherman fled from the hall, back down the towering corridors of the palace to where he found the pine forest again. The pearl was lodged safely beneath his arm.

He ran and ran, but soon realized he was going round in circles.

'However do I get home?' he puzzled. Without pausing to work out a solution, he simply went on running, feeling sure that at some time he would arrive somewhere.

Just as he had hoped, he felt the warmth of the midday sun upon his back. He took off his oilskin coat and wiped the sweat

from his brow. He was on dry land again; the land of his home
and Emperor.

Needless to say, it was to the Emperor's palace that he
began to walk.

Now seeing this rather shabby person at their gates, the
guards were not exactly willing to let him through.

'What do you mean you've got something for him?'

'I mean what I say,' said the fisherman. 'I mean I have this,
if you must know,' and at that he raised his arm and showed
the guards the large pearl that was hidden at his side.

He was then hustled to the court, though at every stage he
was questioned and refused until he showed his wonderful
treasure. At last he stood in the imperial throne-room. The
fisherman had never actually seen the Emperor face to face
before, and therefore was not sure which one of all the grand
elegantly-dressed men he was. They all glowered at the
fisherman. They sat in rows of seats, each raised one above the
other. There were benches in front of each row and on these
were scrolls of paper, pens and menacing looking instruments.

'They say you have a pearl for me,' said a voice; the voice of
the man who sat upon a feathered throne in the centre of the
platform of seats.

'Oh yes, your Majesty,' (the fisherman guessed this was the
Emperor; well, it was obvious, really, now he came to think of
it). 'I was in my boat and went a bit far. I leaned over and I fell
into this hill that I'd seen. I fell into a hole, you see. Then there
was this marvellous place, like a forest palace. And there were
trees and walls of jade. And there was a black dragon who was
guarding the pearl, and when he started sneezing, I took it and
ran away.'

At first there was a silence throughout the throne-room.
Then peals of laughter broke out amongst the assembled
company. From every place at every height the men held their
faces, coughing and spluttering, laughing fit to burst.

'I see,' said the Emperor, who couldn't avoid a grin himself. 'And where is this pearl?'

'Here it is,' said the fisherman, fumbling in his oilskin until he held it out at arm's length in the palm of his hand.

Something fell to the ground. It was a measuring device that had been picked up by one of the noblemen as he moved in his seat. He was going to come forward to inspect the pearl, but instead he fell back in the arms of the man next to him and the instrument dropped, leaving a resounding echo amidst an uncanny silence.

'Good gracious!' declared the Emperor.

'What? What's the matter?' asked the bewildered fisherman.

'Why that type of pearl is well known, but has never actually been found. It was documented in the imperial archives centuries ago. They say its rays may reach thousands of miles, the width of China itself. And as long as it shines in the sun, wherever those rays fall, no wind, no rain, no fire, nor thunder, not even war itself may reign. They say it renders even the most poisonous of serpents quite harmless.'

'Really? Then I'm very glad I found it.'

A buzz of whispers scattered through the hall. The noise grew to exclamation and eventually to uninterrupted shouting.

'It cannot be the same!'

'Not found by an ignorant fisher!'

'It needs careful consideration; do not believe him!'

'Hush, hush,' pleaded the Emperor, and turning to the fisherman he continued. 'You do realize that what you have found, if it is the same type of pearl, is better than any defence my learned ministers might care to propose for this country?'

'Is it? No, I didn't.'

'And as such, it is essential we should check the validity of what you say, what you claim. Where did you say you had found it?'

'In the sea.'

The buzz rose again and the Emperor raised his hand to silence it.

'I have here all the best-esteemed professors of my land. Here amongst others are astronomers, geographers and oceanographers. My men of science will need proof, nothing short of proof, that your story is true.'

'You mean they want to see the underwater kingdom too?'

A single gasp rang out from the mouths of the astonished audience.

'Er – yes, I suppose that is an idea,' said the Emperor.

'But we shall have to make great plans,' said one professor.

'And time – we need the time to do this in,' said another.

'Then I shall give you time. You have until next week,' the Emperor declared, and he came down from his throne and took the fisherman by the arm, inviting him to tea in his private apartments where he hoped he could inspect the pearl without undue fuss.

A week later the learned professors said they were as ready for the expedition as they would ever be. The Emperor himself accompanied them in an imperial barge, big enough to hold all their equipment. This included four hundred roasted swallows, dragon vapour in case the beast found swallows indigestible, and the essence of green-coloured wood. Forty bearers they took with them, to guard the load they carried.

When they approached the vicinity where the fisherman believed he had stopped, the Emperor said to his company:

'Write it down. We are in the Sea of Dunting. Have each stage of this mission, each observation, each speculation recorded exactly as they occur, marking the precise time and the conditions under which they were first made.'

'We shall, your Imperial Highness. Our word must be considered more plausible than that of this fisher.'

The fisherman was not listening to his fellow explorers. He was leaning over the side of the barge, searching the waters with his eyes.

'Yes, it's there. The green hill with the hole in it.'

47

The barge almost overturned in the sea as every member on board raced to where the fisherman stood.

'Mark the spot, its exact latitude and longitude,' said the geographer.

'And place a pole here, so that at night-time we may judge its position in relation to the moon,' said the astronomer.

'Drop a line and measure the distance between the surface of the water and the point where the hole begins,' said the oceanographer.

'Well, are you going to follow me?' asked the fisherman as he prepared to jump in the water.

'Er – I have to stay and make notes,' said one man.

'And my great-grandson once slew a hundred dragons which makes my family an enemy of the species for ever,' said another.

'Um – I suffer from a peculiar malady which makes me come out in spots if ever I approach a reptile,' said one more.

The fisherman was naturally disappointed by their timidity and the Emperor, seeing this, and being a little ashamed of his men of science, commanded that they follow.

Muttering and complaining, holding their noses, clinging to their instruments and devices, the learned company dropped one by one through the hole of the green hill, after the fisherman.

He led them through the circling pine-forest where the geographer and oceanographer held up the expedition for almost an hour in an attempt to count the trees around them.

'And worthwhile to work out the varying relations between each circle's circumference. . . .' they mused.

The fisherman led them to the walls of the jade palace, through its corridors, to the vast central chamber where the astrologer tried to calculate the distance between its almost unseen roof and the nearest star. And at each interruption the fisherman sighed which only served to annoy each scientist.

'How dare he show such disrespect. He is a nobody. He has no knowledge,' they said between them.

48

But they saw the dragon sitting coiled round another pearl, just as the fisherman had described. Now they must admit I am right, he thought, as he stood watching them talking together.

'Well? Is he going to sneeze?'

'Of course not. Dragons cannot sneeze; their facial and nasal muscles do not allow for such spontaneous action.'

'Besides he looks hardly in a sneezing mood; he looks rather menacing.'

They soon stopped their talking. They watched the great, black dragon rear to its feet and move towards them. They shrieked and swore but were soon silenced when the dragon opened wide its mouth and gulped them down its throat in a single, massive swallow.

The fisherman, his eyes on the pearl, luckily had run round the back of the dragon and under its wide wings, then round beneath its very neck to claim the treasure once again. When he realized what had happened to the imperial scientists he was, of course, horrified, and could only stand staring up at the dragon's twitching nostrils.

The beast's front claw began to wave. It flung back its head in agony. Its eyes were streaming with tears.

'It's something about me,' said the fisherman aloud though no one was near to record what he had surmised. He looked down at what he was wearing.

'That's it – that's what it is. The dragon simply doesn't like the smell of my oilskin coat.'

As if almost to confirm what the fisherman had said, the dragon let out an enormous sneeze, and with it, the company of imperial scientists were flung back to the marble floor.

Back at the palace, some days later, the Emperor began his speech. A grand reception was taking place for the fisherman who was to be received into the Ministry of Imperial Scientific Advisers. A seat was made for him on that platform in the throne-room where he had first been allowed into the Emperor's presence.

'. . . and it is with great pleasure and esteem that we welcome amongst us this man whose extraordinary powers we can only submit to and appreciate in untold admiration.'

He wasn't sure, but the fisherman thought he heard odd grunting noises coming from the benches surrounding him.

'. . . we therefore make him Chief Scientist of the Realm, leader of all expeditions and the Curator of the Imperial Museum. . . . '

So that is what this tale amounts to. The fisherman received far more than he ever dreamed was due to him. And often, when alone, when he was not being asked the solution to some elaborate, academic inquiry (a situation he tried to avoid, though he was usually applauded when he gave what was to him the obvious response) he would amble past the glass cases in the museum.

There he stared for long hours at the two orange-sized pearls that were locked up, only occasionally being taken out into the sun to have their rays spread out across the broad land. There too he saw his oilskin coat, and laughed to himself that he now had little opportunity of wearing it. His new, flamboyant robes were identical to those of the other professors.

But since he had in his possession the keys to all the cabinets there, he sometimes took the oilskin from its stand in the museum and secretly went out in his small boat to visit the green hill, the pine forest, the jade palace and the dragon. There were other pearls, but he didn't see the point of taking them away with him. He merely made the journey and returned without telling a soul; just for the fun of it.

6

The Seal Fisher
and the Roane

FAR, far in the north of Scotland, by the sea, lived a man who earned his living by fishing. One morning, as he was out in his boat, he saw a seal swimming towards him.

'I could get a fine price for a good sealskin,' he thought, and he leapt up excitedly, hoping to see not one, but perhaps many more seals. He speared the seal, but the wounded animal swerved and swam away carrying his knife with it. The fisherman returned home, saddened at losing such an opportunity.

That night, as he sat at his table eating a good, hot supper, a knock sounded at the door. The fisherman rose and went outside, thinking it was rather late for people to be calling. At first he could see no one in the darkness, but then he saw a man with a horse at his side. The man had obviously ridden a long way for he was breathless. The fisherman was about to invite him in, but the stranger clung to the horse's reins and seemed in a hurry.

'I have been sent by someone else,' said the stranger. 'Someone who would buy many sealskins from you, someone who would see you – tonight.'

'Really?' asked the delighted fisherman who was already taking off his napkin. His supper could wait.

'Come up on my horse, behind me,' said the stranger, and soon the two of them were riding fast into the night. On and on they went as the wind blew in their faces and the cold night air wrapped itself around their bodies. The fisherman wondered where he was being taken. He could see no house for miles, only the sea and the cliffs to one side and the rising dark hills on the other. The horse galloped faster and the fisherman grew frightened. He clung to the stranger with all his might until he could keep silent no longer.

'Hey – I say! Where does this man live?' he exclaimed, and he noticed that the horse was now slowing down to a trot.

'You'll soon see,' said the stranger.

They were now standing on the edge of a high precipice and beneath them the waves howled and smacked the rocks. And here the stranger told the fisherman to dismount.

'But where – '

The fisherman had little time to ask questions for the stranger suddenly grabbed his arm and pushed him and together they plunged headlong into the sea. Down, down, down. They went down until they reached the very bottom. The fisherman was quite dazed and thought it a miracle that he hadn't drowned. He blinked and saw, hidden in the surface of a rock, a door. It opened and the stranger urged him to follow. Soon the fisherman found himself in a large, dry cave, one of many, so it seemed. He could stand here; he could breathe as well, quite easily. The air was clear and fresh. And then he looked around. There they were – seals, countless numbers of them and oddly enough they seemed to be watching him. But why?

He looked at himself and was alarmed to find that he too was almost transformed into a seal. Then he understood. This was the Kingdom of the Roanes, those mild, magical beings who think and feel and live beneath the sea. The Roanes: they swim with the skins of seals between this space below and the earth above. At other times they seem like ordinary people, like himself. He recognized the stranger again. He was

carrying a knife and came towards him. Was he going to kill him? And yet the Roanes were not angry, they seemed so quiet, so sad.

'Do you know this knife?' asked the stranger.

The fisherman knew it well, he could not deny it. It was that same knife that had killed so many seals, the knife he had lost that very morning. Were they going to punish him now? Was that why he had been brought here?

'The seal you speared today was my father,' said the stranger. 'He lies dangerously ill and only you can save him, if you will.'

'Oh I will, I will!' cried the fisherman and he saw many large seal eyes staring up at him, waiting, hoping.

'Come then,' said the stranger, and the fisherman followed obediently, walking through deep, echoing corridors of stone. At last they came to an open, well-lit space where several Roanes attended the gasping body of a seal that lay prone on a smooth rock. The red stains on its back marked the spot where the fisherman had speared it. Looking at it now he felt ashamed, he wanted to do something that might make the seal better, but before they approached, the stranger spoke to the fisherman.

'Forgive me for lying to you at your cottage. You will know that there is no person, no order for sealskins at all. But I had to bring you here somehow. He's my father – '

The fisherman understood the pain he had caused the Roanes.

'I'm so sorry. You must tell me what to do,' he replied.

The stranger led him to the wounded seal and instructed him and the fisherman laid his hands upon the bleeding flesh when, almost at once, it began to heal. The skin was clean and healthy again, smooth and shining. The seal leapt up and barked his joy and all the Roanes cheered till the caves echoed with noise and laughter. Then the stranger led the fisherman back through the corridors.

'I will lead you home now, but first,' he said, 'you must

make a solemn vow. You must swear never to kill a single seal ever again.'

The fisherman hung his head. 'You have treated me kindly,' he said, 'though I have taken so many of you and sold your skins for money. Still you are good to me. I promise never to harm you again.'

With that the stranger clutched the fisherman and led him back up into the sea. Up and up to the wild, stormy waves they went and with a huge leap they reached the top of the cliffs. Then the stranger breathed on the fisherman and they both became men again. They looked to see the horse nearby, munching the soft grass in the cool moonlight as if nothing could disturb him, as if nothing had happened since they were last there. They rode back, the wind in their faces, the night air blowing all around them until they came at last to the cottage door. The fisherman peered inside and noticed his supper, now cold, on the table, the napkin he had flung aside in his urgent desire to follow the stranger, to gain wealth from the skins of seals. He'd never be rich now.

The stranger tapped the fisherman's shoulder and from beneath his cloak he produced a green bag. He gave it to the fisherman, saying:

'Take this present. The fish you catch will not bring you enough to live on, but if you use what lies in here, carefully, you will not want for more.'

The fisherman peered inside the bag and thought he saw a twinkling of light, a gold colour, and as he raised his eyes to thank him, he saw that the stranger had gone and was riding back, along the clifftops to the sea.

7

Taufatahi
and Fakapatu

or *Why Sharks Never Attack*
the Men of Moungaone

In a cave on the island of Tofua lived Taufatahi, one of the most enormous and loud-mouthed giants that ever lived. The sharks of the ocean quivered when they heard him roar his orders, for he was their lord and whatever he commanded, they knew they should obey him.

Not far away, at Moungaone, another giant roamed the shore, basking in the hot sunshine, occasionally staring out at the wide, blue sea. Fakapatu was his name. He would have loved to have gone for a swim when the sweat streamed from his brow like mountain waterfalls, when his huge eyes blinked and the weight of his body seemed hard to carry across the sands to his own cave. But he was afraid of the sea and all the sharks that lurked there.

The two giants knew about each other and often were able to meet. Taufatahi, so keen to rule beyond the territory of his own water, resented Fakapatu's lovely home. And Fakapatu envied the opportunity Taufatahi had of being free to swim wherever he chose, without fearing for his life. Whenever they met, a fight almost certainly ensued.

Now one day, having sent his sharks on a marathon swim, and with little else to do, Taufatahi decided it might be good sport to visit his neighbour. He was not one to enjoy the calm of a hot afternoon. He waded towards Moungaone and began his search. As he passed a cave, he heard from deep within its hollow, cool darkness, a voice that sounded very familiar. It was Fakapatu talking to himself.

'Come out here!' bellowed Taufatahi. 'Let's see if you're as great as me.'

Annoyed at the intrusion on his peace, Fakapatu emerged from his cave, hoping to send off Taufatahi with a few smart words. But it seemed there was no one there.

'That's most strange,' he said, 'I'm sure that was Taufatahi's voice.'

Immediately he heard a laugh that came from the gaping mouth of a small fish on the sand.

'Yes, it's me,' it chuckled. 'It's Taufatahi. I've turned myself into a fish. I don't suppose you could do that,' he said provocatively. 'Oh no, you're a big, bloated pudding of a giant.'

'As a matter of fact I don't much want to,' replied Fakapatu. 'The way you talk seems quite unnecessary and stupid to me. If you're not careful I shall eat you.'

Taufatahi realized his performance was not having much effect. He changed himself back to his normal, colossal size. Then suddenly he became most fearfully alarmed. Fakapatu, imitating his foolery, had also turned into a fish, but instead of wriggling on the sand where he could so easily be trodden on and crushed in an instant, he leapt into Taufatahi's mouth. Quite involuntarily Taufatahi swallowed him.

A wave of disappointment overcame the giant as he wandered along the shore. Fakapatu was gone. Where else would he find someone of his own size on whom he could play tricks? How would he spend his empty hours when, tired of bullying his sharks, the idea of taunting his neighbour seemed so delightful? There was a limit to the entertainment he could find alone.

Thinking this way, and a little despondent, he began to feel rather sick.

'It must be because of my sorrow,' he told himself.

But the feeling did not go. What had started as a vague, hollow sensation now grew into a definite pain. He felt his stomach expand. Then his ribs began to hurt. He stood still a moment.

'No – no it cannot be,' he cried aloud.

He realized that Fakapatu, far from being lost to him, was in fact beginning to resume his normal shape *inside* him.

'Stop! Stop! You'll kill me this way. I only ever wanted to have some fun with you.'

But the swelling increased. Taufatahi thought he would soon explode.

'I will give you anything you want,' he cried; 'my land, my entire territory, my cave. Only do stop!'

A voice, rather suffocated, came from Taufatahi's throat.

'I don't want your land, nor your cave. Mine are good enough.'

'What then? What can I do for you?'

'You rule the sharks of the sea, do you not?' asked Fakapatu.

'Yes, yes. Do you want them? You can have them, gladly.'

'I don't want them. In fact I think they're beastly. Everyone on Moungaone hates them. We fear them, not you.'

'Well, I'll do anything you say. But oh – stop this pain. Stop it!'

'Tell your sharks to leave my people and the shores of Moungaone. Tell them.'

'All right then, if I must.'

The great giant widened a little more.

'Tell them now,' said Fakapatu. 'And when I've seen that you've done this, I shall come out.'

And so, writhing with the hurt that seemed at last to be strangulating his very heart, Taufatahi faced the sea and looked over to his own land, Tofua. He called, as best he could, and soon the deep blue ocean was dotted about with sharp, erect, black specks; the tails of his countless sharks.

'Hear me you subjects, my sharks. Hear me when I tell you that never are you to taunt the people of Moungaone, nor even approach its shores. And this must be not only in my time, but in the time of all my descendants and those who live on Moungaone in the future.'

The black tails bobbed up and down in the rippling sea as if to say, 'Yes – we will obey you.'

The exasperated Taufatahi, who had nearly lost all power of speech, then croaked, 'Was that what you wanted?'

In reply to his question, Fakapatu leapt from Taufatahi's mouth, shuddered and resumed his full size, standing there before Taufatahi on the sand. And Taufatahi collapsed with a mixture of relief and exhaustion.

The people of Moungaone now say it is perfectly safe to swim beyond the reef of their island. Ever since their own giant took his first happy steps into the water, the sharks from Tofua have always kept their distance, remembering what was commanded them, once, long ago.

8

The Angry Merwife
of Nordstrand

THERE was once a busy merwife (not a mermaid; even mermaids marry and become merwives) and she lived out in Nordstrand. Each morning she drove her cattle from her home in the sea to a small meadow, Tibirke Mark. Then she would sit peacefully as they grazed and think out the rest of her daily routine.

Now the people of Tibirke did not take kindly to her. As with anyone who is a little different, the merwife became the centre of attention and gossip. And all she wanted to do was to give her cows some nourishing food: the grass that could not be found in the sea.

'Oh, but have you seen the way she walks?' some would say about the merwife. 'Sort of wriggling but with short steps. There's no one has seen an actual tail, but it must be there. She's not like the rest of us.'

'No, and since she's not like the rest of us, why should she use our land?'

The more they talked, the more they gathered together to discuss her, the more they were determined to make her life difficult.

Eventually, they thought of a plan and hoped it would send her from their village for ever. They waited, early in the

60

morning, to hear the sound of the shell bells round the necks of her cattle. They knew she would be coming from the sea. They lined themselves up on her usual route so that, as she shuffled towards them, she was bound to stop.

'There she is. I hear the shell bells and the snorting of the cows' nostrils. She is coming,' one said.

As she approached, her cattle before her, she did indeed falter. She stared at them in silence and this served only to annoy them. Then they moved. They faced her and placed one foot before the other, slowly at first, but then at a steady pace until the cows staggered sideways and the merwife's awkward lilt almost caused her to fall.

The people of Tibirke drove the cows and the merwife every morning to a public enclosure. And once there they questioned and cajoled her and insisted that she, like everyone else, should pay the fixed price for pasturage.

'But I have none of your money. I have no need of money in the sea.'

'You must. Or else stay in the sea!' they exclaimed.

The merwife's pale eyes turned deep blue as she watched them. She felt their animosity and grew angry herself. But she contained the desire to shout back.

'I have no money,' she repeated slowly.

After several mornings they saw that their plan was failing and they wondered what to do next.

'Well we must win. We could get something from her instead of money. We cannot look fools.'

The next day, the merwife approached the shore and began her usual walk towards the open meadow, though she knew it was likely her path would be barred by the villagers. There they stood and this time again she controlled the anger in her heart. Her blue eyes flashed and a smile spread across her face. They steered the cattle to the enclosure, and the merwife found herself surrounded by the all too familiar faces.

'We must have something from you,' the villagers called.

'Then you may have the precious girdle that encircles my body,' said the merwife.

Their mouths fell open. They could hardly believe what they heard. They stopped and looked at the bands of gilded cloth studded with gems of varying shapes and sizes. Eagerly, they tore the girdle from her body and soon were able to forget all about the merwife and her cattle.

As she drove them back towards the shore, it seemed the merwife was talking secretly to her cows. Then, quite emphatically, she addressed a single beast.

'Rake up now!' she exclaimed, and with its short horns the cow threw up the sand from the shore until it spread all along the coast, beyond the dunes, in a misty whirlwind. A strong breeze blew from the north-west, across the sea where the merwife had her home. The sand flew and swirled over to the village of Tibirke, so that even the church was covered until only its spire showed above the buried buildings, towering like a needle pointing to heaven.

And what of the villagers? Before the sandstorm engulfed their homes, they took the precious girdle to the square where everyone could see what was the reward for their treatment of the merwife. People clamoured to view the famous girdle. But they fell back in horror, for it was made of worthless seaweed, and sticking to the tendrils were scores of common sea shells and limpets.

The angry merwife drove her cattle beneath the sea, then back upon another stretch of land, to a place where she hoped her task would be welcomed. And never again was she heard of on the Nordstrand shores.

9

Urashima Taro

IF you were to live in a small village by the sea, you would soon grow to know almost everything about everyone who lived there. The place itself would become very familiar. Beyond the few houses, that large expanse of water would provide work and food enough to keep body and soul alive. Would there be need of anything else in life?

Urashima Taro, a young fisher boy, was very happy living simply by his work, greeting his neighbours, enjoying the company of friends and family. Some said he was the most popular person in all Japan; others knew he was certainly the best loved of the village in which he lived. His warmth and understanding and, above all, his kindness never failed to impress even the meanest of souls.

One evening, pleased with his day's catch, Urashima Taro decided to amble through the narrow streets before retiring to bed. It was a pleasant, warm night. His peace, however, was soon disturbed by the sounds of jeers and laughter and the sight of young ruffians kicking something at their feet. On coming closer, he saw they were tormenting a helpless turtle.

'Stop! Stop I say,' he implored them, but they took no notice of him. 'Here – I'll buy you sweets; I'll give you what you like only do stop this cruelty.'

The boys eyed him with caution and Urashima Taro, seeing they were not averse to the promise of gifts, offered to buy the turtle from them as if it were their own. The suggestion was greeted gladly and soon Urashima Taro was left alone with the poor creature.

'I'll take you back to the sea, my friend,' he whispered, as he carefully cradled it in his arms. 'For if you meet with ruffians like that again, how will you live your thousand years or more?'

He stood on the sand as he watched the turtle creep slowly into the lapping waves and he did not regret the loss of his hard-earned money.

The next day, with the sky overhead clear and blue and the promise of tugs at his line, Urashima Taro put out to sea with a cheerful heart. He was staring out at the straight, brilliant horizon when he heard his name being called. He looked round but could see no one near. Then he heard a knock, a tap on the side of his boat. There, in the water, was a turtle – surely the same one he had found, for he recognized its eyes, its large, round eyes.

'I want to thank you for your kindness,' said the turtle. 'I wonder, could you lift me into your boat?'

'But of course,' replied the delighted Urashima Taro, who was deeply moved by the sweet tones of the turtle's voice.

'Thank you,' it said as it settled on his lap. 'And I wonder – I don't suppose – I feel sure you won't have travelled far. Am I right?'

'Yes, quite right. I'm happy enough here. Why do you ask?'

'It's just that by way of gratitude, since you saved my life, I thought you might like to visit the Palace of Rin-Jin with me. You've not been there, I know that.'

'Rin-Jin!' exclaimed the astonished Urashima Taro. 'Why Rin-Jin is the Dragon-King of the Sea. How can I visit that place?'

'I shall take you. Oh, it has walls of pearl whose light

changes with each tide that touches them. And the weeds and plants of the deep are woven into trellis and vine. They cover the garden walks through which the royal entourage . . . .'

'Stop! Wait. How can I go there? Your words thrill me with delight, but your plan is in vain. I have never made such a journey and you – you are too small to carry me.'

No sooner had he said this than the turtle began to grow. It almost toppled onto the planks of Urashima Taro's boat. Back in the water again, it encouraged Urashima Taro to hold tight to its great, firm shell. Though he was momentarily struck with misgivings, Urashima Taro couldn't resist the chance of seeing all that the turtle described.

He was not disappointed. Deep down past the darkest regions of the ocean, the shade dispersed and a glimmering light of green and blue hung round the gold sea-bed. He saw before him a wondrous palace rising up through the swirling, pale waters. The gates were of crystalline stone that sparkled and shone like diamonds, and on either side huge pillars stood firm, though the light made them appear to flicker and dance.

'We have arrived,' said the turtle, and no sooner had it spoken than the gates were thrown open to welcome them. Another turtle, a messenger, led the way through long, marble corridors, the floors and walls of which were flecked with all the colours of the sea. High above, great chandeliers of sea shells tinkled and spun as the spellbound Urashima Taro gasped with wonder and followed the turtle.

At last they reached the hall of the Dragon-King. Urashima Taro stopped as he beheld the rows of elegant courtiers all circling round the pure white walls. He felt moved to enter, to kneel before the splendid throne where Rin-Jin sat in majesty. At once a loud peal of voices rang from all sides:

'Hail to he who comes from the land of the Rising Sun.'

As he peered up at the Dragon-King's throne, he saw that Rin-Jin smiled and raised his hand in welcome. And beside him was another figure, a young girl, crowned like the King with coral and pearls.

'We have heard you are the kindest man in Japan,' Rin-Jin announced. 'Tell us all about yourself.'

'Oh yes, but oh – what a wonderful place. I came on the back of a turtle, but it has gone. I thought it was – '

'No,' said the girl as she stepped down from the Dragon-King's throne. 'I did not leave you. For I am that same turtle, once under a spell, now happily released by your care.'

She held out her arms to him and as he watched her face he noticed her large, round eyes and knew at once that she spoke the truth.

'I am Rin-Jin's daughter; the Dragon-Princess.'

He knelt again and vowed he would serve the Dragon Court for as long as he was living. 'And dare I ask for the years of a turtle-life, to stay here in this palace for ever with you all?'

His request was granted.

From then on, Urashima Taro lived in splendour and amazement. He was clothed in the finest silks he had ever seen, of colours to compete with the deepest tones of sunset. When he ate, he was served with the sweetest fruits, and wine and spices such as he had never tasted before. The Dragon-King gave him only one command: to hold his court with story-telling, describing the life he once led as a fisherman.

In time, filled with love for the Dragon-Princess, as she was for him, Urashima Taro married and it seemed he had all he ever dared to wish for. As he looked into her eyes he sometimes remembered that evening, so long ago, when he had first seen her mocked and abused. He thought of the time she had called him, out at sea; the morning when the sun was bright and the sky was clear and it seemed that all was well with the world.

One day, as he was describing the intricacies of baiting a hook and the need for silence that followed if a man were to make a good catch, Urashima Taro was struck by an awful thought. He could not speak for a while.

'What is it, my Urashima Taro?' asked the Dragon-Princess.

'My boat. My wooden boat . . . .'

'What of it, Urashima Taro dear?'

'What can have happened to it, I wonder?'

The Dragon-Princess tried to calm him and banish all his fears. She was frightened of the stare that had entered his eyes.

'But my family, my mother; they will think I have drowned,' he said, rising from his couch and ignoring the buzz of whispers that reverberated through the great, white hall.

'I must go back.'

'Don't say so,' said the Dragon-Princess.

'I shall go back, just to visit, just to let them know I am safe,' said Urashima Taro, trying to explain his need and comfort his wife at the same time.

'If it be so, take with you this red box to remember me by,' she replied sadly. 'It will take you there. It will also bring you back. But you must promise me never to open it. For if you were to open it, something dreadful would happen to you.'

'I promise,' said Urashima Taro as he took from her hands the little red lacquer box.

With great sorrow, but kindly understanding, the Dragon-Princess waved Urashima Taro goodbye as he left the huge gates of the Palace. Turning his face upward, his heart beat in anticipation of seeing his old home once more.

When he reached the shore, he noticed the sky was clear and radiant as it had been when he left. He walked towards the village, but almost immediately he saw something was strange about the look of the whole area. The houses were not quite so small nor even facing the beach. And the trees: some were huge, others gone. He had to find his home. When he entered the main street that led to the village centre, he felt he was being eyed by the people passing by. They were laughing at him.

'What makes you so intrigued?' he asked, uneasy at the lack of warmth they showed him.

'It's your clothes,' said one. 'You look very odd.'

Of course, he thought; the splendid clothes of Rin-Jin's court. But as he glanced at his sleeves he saw he wore the threadbare tunic he had always worn as a fisherman.

'But it is I – Urashima Taro. I've come back to say I'm safe.'

'Urashima Taro! Urashima Taro!' they cried, with smirks of unkind laughter. 'You mean Urashima Taro the fisher boy, the one who was swallowed by a turtle?'

'Yes, yes – at least I was not swallowed. The turtle was a princess.'

'A likely tale! What a crazy man!'

'It's true. It's true. And I am Urashima Taro.'

Then one man, approaching him with bold, measured steps, touched his arms and hair.

'You seem real enough. But Urashima Taro, the fisher boy, lived four hundred years ago. They found his boat and they saw the marks of the turtle. His story has become a legend, a warning not to dream, nor be soft-hearted.'

Urashima Taro stood bewildered as he saw them walk away, still laughing, occasionally looking back over their shoulders at him. He then began the search for his parents' house, but where the bamboo walls once had stood, he found another, strange, stony construction. He felt completely desolate.

He wondered if he had indeed been dreaming. Was the Palace of the Dragon-King real? Was he dreaming now? As he drifted from place to place, longing for some sign of recognition, he became more and more lonely, hoping he would soon wake up and find himself back in his former life with the village as it used to be. Then he had treasured each simple moment and never asked for more. But the Princess! The red lacquer box was still in his hand. He couldn't forget her and he longed to be with her again.

He sat on the shore and watched the waves and the sea that he hoped contained her. He saw behind him the fishing-boats and the people at work and still he was not sure that he might not find his home if he looked again. Then he stared at the red box.

'I have to open it, for nothing that happens can be worse than this present confusion.'

As he lifted the lid, a delicate, sweet fragrance banished the smell of salt from his nose. He felt a tingling in his toes and fingers; it moved up his legs and arms. When he looked down he saw his skin had begun to wither and wrinkle into dry folds. He took a step towards the sea, but his bones cracked and he stumbled.

'Oh, my Princess. I should have trusted you, but I have been so muddled since I sought my home again. I should have stayed with you,' he cried, as he fell on the sand in pain.

Lying there, he was just able to see a pale, purple mist rising from the centre of the small box. It hung in the air above him. When his eyes closed he heard the voice of the turtle, the Dragon-Princess. It called and it moaned as the mist grew thin and hovered above him, spreading further away across the sea till it vanished.

10

Why the Sea Moans

A CASTLE stood on high land. Its turrets pointed firm and sharp into the sky; its tall windows faced the rose-bed gardens where low hedges lined each pleasant walk that surrounded its sheer, ochre walls. A happy child might skip and play through these castle grounds to her heart's content, but the young Princess was not happy; she was lonely. She wandered slowly, staring at her feet as they crunched the pebble walkways, past the silent, stone statues on every side.

'If you could live and talk, I might find among you one friend,' she complained, as she meandered towards the terrace steps. There she looked out into the distance, for her a vast expanse containing nothing and no one. There the sea stretched out to meet the sky and she was comforted to think that, in its breadth and emptiness, it too might be lonely. It was her favourite part of the garden. She often ran down to the shore. There she listened to the waves.

'Dionysia, Dionysia . . . .' they seemed to be saying, and this was her name. She was glad of the call for then she knew she might talk.

'Not one friend but the sea. I meet many people from the court, the dukes and counts, the ladies and their waiting-maids. But amongst them all I have not a single friend.'

'Dionysia, Dionysia – I am your friend,' came the sound, only this time it seemed so much stronger than before. She stared into the ebbing water. Beneath the breaking waves, a sea-serpent crawled its way onto the sand.

She started back.

'Do not be afraid of me, Dionysia,' said the sea-serpent and on looking close into its eyes, the princess was soon calmed.

'Who are you, that you should be able to talk?' she said.

'Have you not heard me calling you? I speak your name time and again. I have a name too. I am called Labismena.'

From that day on, the Princess was rarely lonely. At every opportunity, when she could escape her royal duties, she would gladly run to the shore to talk and play with the sea-serpent. If ever other people walked by, the creature disappeared, and they would see Dionysia tiptoeing the sand, splashing along the margin of the water.

'How she loves to be here, although it is so wild,' they remarked, never guessing her real motive. 'But she is growing into a lady. She cannot always play.'

It was true; Dionysia soon passed the years of childhood and was requested, more than ever before, to attend the grand, royal functions that frequently took place in the castle. But still she preferred to be with Labismena.

One day, as they sat together and talked, Labismena spoke with a note of sadness in her voice.

'Dionysia, I too am older. We are past the years of games. And you will have to leave my company soon. I want you to know that if you are ever in trouble, you need only come and seek me out and I shall help you. The years we have spent on this sea-shore shall never be forgotten by me.'

'And nor by me,' said Dionysia, a little afraid of the prospect of their parting. She didn't want to be lonely again.

Meanwhile, in another country, a queen lay dying. She was distressed to think of her husband having no one beside him whom he could call his wife. She gave him her wedding-ring and said:

'Whoever has a finger to fit this ring should become your next Queen. It must be neither too tight nor too loose. It should slip onto her finger as easily as if it had been made for her.'

When the Queen died, the King began his search.

In the castle by the sea every member of the royal household from bewigged courtier to scullery maid, gossiped and prattled and joked, and hoped that their own Dionysia would find that the ring fitted her. Sixteen, they thought, was a perfect age to be married to a King.

But Dionysia had other ideas. In her lone hours in the gardens or wandering by the sea-shore, hoping for a glimpse of her old friend Labismena, she had taken to dreaming of a young man, some prince who would take her away from all she had come to dislike about her home. She knew what her family hoped for her.

'Oh, that I should marry that beastly old man!' she cried, as she stamped her feet in temper.

The King came to the castle, bringing with him his royal entourage and the ring itself.

Proudly, Dionysia's father assembled his court in the state reception rooms and, from his raised throne, he commanded that Dionysia, sitting a few steps below him, should hold out her left hand for the trial. She trembled in anticipation. The old King slipped the ring on her finger. It was neither too tight nor too loose; it fitted exactly. Dionysia struggled to hold back her enormous dismay, but she burst into tears.

'Dionysia! How dare you be so ungrateful. This should be a moment of celebration for us all, especially for you. You see before you your future husband.'

'Never!' she cried.

The people who were gathered round gasped with alarm.

The King, her father, rose from his throne; his face was red with anger.

'What are you saying child?'

'I'm saying he is no such thing.'

In the days that followed, Dionysia refused to eat. She sat at the long dining-table and stared at the food before her that grew cold and nasty until it was quite inedible. Her parents, seeing this, were considerably annoyed.

'Make the wedding date earlier than we planned!' they declared, fearing she would look too thin and unwell when all their guests came to see the ceremony.

Ill she almost became, but as Dionysia watched from her window, wondering how she could escape the dreaded day, her eyes fell on the distant sea and she remembered the last words Labismena had spoken to her:

'If you are ever in trouble, you need only come and seek me out and I shall help you.'

As she flew down the steps of her turret, as she sped through the echoing corridors, as she leapt from the gates of the castle door to the gardens and terrace outside, the footmen and the maids and the royal family itself thought she had gone quite mad. She ran to the sea-shore and called the name of her old friend.

' . . . oh please come for I am in trouble now!'

True to her word, Labismena wriggled through the foam to the sand, just as she had done before. She was thrilled to see Dionysia again.

'Ah, how good it is to be with you,' said the sea-serpent. 'How long I have been alone, wondering what your days bring you.'

'Listen Labismena, it's completely horrible what my days bring me. It is an old man, a king, who is to marry me. But I won't have it, I won't! I want a young man, a prince with whom I shall fall in love.'

'I understand,' said Labismena to Dionysia's plea. 'Then I suggest we make things difficult. But tell me Dionysia, have you never thought of me 'til now?'

'I've had so much to think of. I lead a very busy life.'

'Of course you do. This is what I suggest. Tell your father you will marry the King only – '

'But I will not marry the King!'

'Listen to me. Trust me. It shall never happen.'

'Go on then, tell me.'

'Say to your father you will marry the King only when he has brought you a dress of the colours of all the fields and all the flowers of the world.'

'What a marvellous idea! Thank you, Labismena,' said Dionysia, and she turned and ran to the castle steps, eager to impart her command.

Labismena crept quietly back into the sea.

When the old King heard what she desired, he immediately left to begin his long journey across all the lands of the world. He knew the people of his own country and those of Dionysia's would delight in the spectacle of such a wedding and all that it meant for them. But for himself it was not a public matter; he deeply loved Dionysia. Had the ring not slipped so easily onto her finger, he would still have chosen her. He was determined to overcome any obstacle that lay in his path and he believed that through his loving her, she would grow to love him. He travelled through many countries and eventually, after some months, he returned with a dress of the colours of all the fields and all the flowers he had seen. He spread it across the floor for all to see.

'No, no!' cried Dionysia on seeing it. Her father called after her when she ran from the grand reception rooms, down to the sea-shore, crying with bitter rage.

'Labismena, Labismena! Come here as quick as you can!' she called.

The sea-serpent wriggled to the shore with the incoming waves.

'My dear Dionysia. What is troubling you now?'

'He found it! He found it! The dress you described. It was not an impossible task after all. Think of something else.'

'Tell him to bring you a dress the colour of all the seas and all the fish that swim in them,' said Labismena. 'But tell me, had you thought I would let you down?'

Dionysia did not answer. She was already on her way back to the castle.

The old King, hearing her new command, prepared for another journey, this time to be taken by ship, across the world. It was not long before he returned, bringing with him a dress the colour of all the seas he had visited, and all the fish that swam there. He laid it proudly before the royal family.

'It cannot be true,' screeched Dionysia, seeing the dress next to that of the colours of all the fields and flowers. Her father, the King, grinned with private glee.

'It *is* true, my girl. Now will you settle to your new responsibilities?'

'Never!' she replied, and she ran away down to the sea-shore as fast as her legs would take her.

'Labismena! Where are you? Come quickly!'

As the waves ascended the beach, so with them came the sea-serpent.

'What has worried you this time, Dionysia?'

'That dress, the second one: he has found it and I am to marry him for sure. You must help me.'

'I shall always help you if I can. Go back and tell him to flnd you a dress that is coloured like the sky at all times of the day and dotted here and there with the sparkling glow of the night-time stars,' said Labismena. 'But Dionysia, would you have come to me had he not found the dress?'

Dionysia did not hear her question; she had fled from the beach anxious to impart her new request.

When the old King heard her, he did not complain but summoned his courtiers to prepare for a journey that would take them to the highest mountains of the world, from where he could reach the sky.

Dionysia waited for his return, staring from her high window, hoping he would not succeed. For after this, she felt there could be no more colours left from which a dress could be made. When she saw his horsemen reach her father's borders, she held her breath in fear.

Down in the great staterooms an official welcome was declared as the old King laid before the throne a dress the colour of the sky in all its daytime and night-time hues and sprinkled over it were tiny, sparkling diamonds.

'There!' cried her father, the King. 'You can continue like this no longer. We shall go ahead with the wedding tomorrow.'

Without saying a word, but with her head held high, Dionysia turned and marched from the assembled crowds, past every face that watched her until she reached the castle grounds. Then she ran. She started calling Labismena's name before she had left the terrace steps, so that by the time her feet touched the sand, she could see the sea-serpent waiting for her.

'Oh, what is to become of me now, Labismena?' she spluttered.

'Tell me the cause of this new sorrow and I will try to help.'

'Oh, you always try, but so far you haven't succeeded. He has come with the third dress. I cannot escape the wedding for it is to be tomorrow.'

'Do not have so little faith in me,' said Labismena. 'Go and bring me the three dresses, now. When you have returned with them I will let you know of the surprise I have planned for you.'

With a gleam of hope dancing in her eyes, Dionysia gladly skipped to her castle turret where she snatched up the three beautiful dresses. People saw her, and thought she had at last decided to accept and welcome the old King as her bridegroom.

'See how she clings to those robes now!' they said.

'And how her face smiles!'

As soon as she was on the beach again, Dionysia stopped suddenly. There, before her, was a ship with its sails unfurled; a ship that had not been there earlier.

'Dionysia, Dionysia!' called Labismena.

'Yes, I'm here. What is all this?'

The sea-serpent bounded and spiralled in the foam.

'Dionysia, this is your escape. Are you not happy?'

78

'I'm not sure.'

'Say you are pleased, for I have been preparing this for you since first you came back to me with your troubles. You shall see all your dreams come true, if you do as I say.'

'But I shall be lonely.'

'Not for long. Board this ship and it will take you far away to the other side of the world. Take only your three dresses. They will come in useful to you when you meet the young Prince who shall claim you for his wife.'

Dionysia could hardly contain her enormous excitement. She jumped and danced upon the sand.

'Oh, how happy I shall be! And no old King and no days alone – not ever again. Oh, how glad I am! How shall I ever thank you?'

'There is a way,' said Labismena.

'Is there? What?'

'Dionysia. You have known me as this serpent for years and years. As a serpent I have waited, listened to and played with you when you needed me. But my needs are great, perhaps greater than yours. For I am not really a sea-serpent. I am a princess like you. The only cure for my loneliness, the only way I can become my real self again, is when the happiest girl in the world remembers me and calls my name three times. You shall be that girl one day. You can release me.'

'Oh, I will, Labismena. What a sad thing it must be to be you. I shall call your name when I'm happy.'

'Don't forget, Dionysia,' said the sea-serpent as the cheerful Princess boarded the ship and began her hopeful voyage.

'I shan't,' she said, waving to her friend.

'Dionysia, Dionysia – don't forget.'

The ship at last came to a land that was obviously very far from Dionysia's home. During the days and nights of the voyage she had become restless and fretful, fearing she might be lonely and in trouble. She wanted to arrive, to meet her Prince and be happy; she did not like having to wait.

As soon as she stepped onto the ground of the new land, the ship vanished and she knew there was no way of returning home.

'What shall I do? Why is the Prince not here to meet me?' she asked herself. Then she began to look for somewhere welcoming and safe where she could rest and collect her thoughts.

'It is obvious I must do what other people do; I must earn my living; I must work. I wonder how they do it?'

She searched from house to house, asking if she might sweep the floors or prepare the meals, but no one seemed to need her. They did it all themselves, they said. Then one day, she heard that a girl was wanted at the royal palace.

'The palace? What an excellent opportunity. I shall go and ask immediately. What is the work?'

'They need a maid to look after the hens.'

Now this might be a daunting task for a princess who was not used to having to work at all, let alone look after hens, but she was pleased to be far away from all her past life when she had been so alone and unhappy, far away from that wedding-day that had been planned.

Dionysia cared well for the royal hens and made a number of companions amongst the palace staff who told her all about their young Prince. But every now and then she envied the royal family their banquets and their balls. In recent years, despite the old King, she had grown to like dressing up.

When she heard there was to be a great feast in the city, she decided she had to go to it.

'I can wear the dress the colour of all the fields and flowers,' she said.

The first day of the feast was held in the palace grounds. Dionysia, wearing the lovely dress, looked quite at home there. People turned their heads to look at her and they wondered who she could be. The Prince himself immediately fell in love with her.

'What a commotion I've caused,' she laughed to herself,

and, enjoying the attention they gave her, she slipped away, back to her hens, so everyone might puzzle further about her.

On the second day of the feast she wore her dress the colour of all the seas and all the fish that swam in them. Again the people stared. Again Dionysia left the feast before dusk.

'She has something about her that is not like ordinary girls,' they said.

The Prince, however, felt he had seen her in the palace farm.

'I'm sure she looks after the hens. I had noticed her before, but never thought to talk to her.'

The Prince sought out Dionysia's friends, the girls who helped with the other animals there.

'Was the girl who looks after the hens at the feast yesterday?' he asked.

'No, no. She was here all evening,' they replied.

'And today; was she not there today, but in different clothing, a beautiful dress also?'

'No, not her. She is with the hens now.'

'I am sure she is the same girl. I will have her for my wife whoever she is.'

The farming girls told Dionysia what he had said and she beamed with joy and pleasure, for she had fallen in love with him. At last, her dreams were coming true, but she wanted the Prince to wait, to know how she had felt, waiting.

For the third day of the feast she put on the dress the colours of the sky at all times and the night-time stars. When the Prince saw her again, he went up to her immediately.

'You are the girl who cares for the royal hens are you not?'

'I am not really a farming girl, no.'

'Whoever you are, I love you. I give you this jewel as a token of my love.'

The Prince left her to think about what he had said. It soon became known that he was unable to eat. The kitchen staff tried to coax him with delicious sweets and sauces, but nothing would he take.

At last, unable to continue with her pretence and knowing the real cause of the Prince's waning appetite, Dionysia evolved a plan whereby she could reveal herself and claim the Prince as her own.

She crept into the kitchens and asked if she might prepare a special broth that was well known in her country. She made the soup (an ordinary mixture of vegetables and meaty bones) and into the tureen she dropped the jewel the Prince had given her.

When he attempted the first mouthful he found the jewel in his spoon.

'Who has made this soup?' he asked, standing at the table in surprise.

'Some girl helping in the kitchens. The girl who looks after the hens.'

Without hesitation he sped to find her. She was waiting at the gate of the royal farm, near to where she worked.

'You are the girl I must marry; but tell me who you are,' he said.

'I am a princess from another land. I have waited so long for you.'

It was with all the pomp and splendour of a thousand feast-days and a thousand royal celebrations that Dionysia and her Prince were married. And on that day she was the happiest girl in the world.

But far out across the sea, a lonely sea-serpent waited for the call she longed to hear. She had waited days, months, years, for her release. She knew the time had at last come.

And when the day ended, she pictured in her mind the happiness and excitement her old friend must be feeling; so happy she had forgotten her promise.

That is why, when you stand still and alone on an empty sea-shore, you can hear the waves moan. You can almost catch the words as the tide moves in and out again:

'Dionysia, Dionysia . . . .'

11

Pelorus Jack

Long, long ago, before the arrival in the Southern Pacific of the white man, when the only boats to be seen upon the clear, blue water were the wooden canoes of the Maori islanders and the bays were dotted here and there with small settlements, it seemed that life would continue always to be peaceful.

But there were two men, living on the shores of Pelorus Sound, who had the misfortune to love the same woman. She was not undecided as to whom she loved the most and when she chose one to be her husband, the other, Ruru, felt he would become quite mad with grief.

He ran along the sands, howling in rage and sorrow. He sprinted over the rocks and up the mountainside until he found her home.

'You shall pay for this choice with your life!' he roared, as he seized her and dragged her outside. Over to the edge of the cliff Ruru carried his once loved, now hated woman. In his anger and without hesitation, he hurled her over the edge. Soon she lay dead on the rocks below.

It so happened that the whole scene had been witnessed from the heights of another cliff.

'Ruru! Ruru!' the observer exclaimed to himself. 'It is Ruru who, in his jealousy, has killed the woman we both loved.' The man, the chosen husband, hurried to the cliff-top incensed with the desire to punish the killer. He flung himself on Ruru, but the madman was already charged with fury that gave him added strength to defend himself against his assailant.

'You shall go the same way as her!' he cried, and he threw his enemy's body over the cliff where it dashed to earth beside the other, still corpse.

Madness did not quite overcome Ruru's brain until the full force of his malign nature swelled and expressed itself in a curse:

'All you gods of the sky, you of the underworld, the sun and the moon and you of the water: conspire together, summon up your strength and tear that man's soul so that it may never find peace. Destroy his spirit; let him wander for eternity in agony and pain. May he never, ever rest.'

The words were uttered as Ruru stood upon the cliff and faced the sea. The words caught the air and rode the waves. A dolphin, sporting and leaping not far from the shore, suddenly fell limp and died; the words of the curse had entered its mind and killed it.

As Ruru watched, his rage began to subside. He saw the great body of the dolphin bob and bounce, lying prone upon the ocean. At last the tide carried it to the shore and when Ruru surveyed the outcome of his terrible condition, the three corpses, he shuddered with fear.

He turned and wandered, dazed, as if still living the nightmare he had created. On reaching his village he sought the tohunga, the holy man of his tribe.

'Help me, please help. I have killed the woman I loved. I have killed the man that she loved. I have invoked the anger of the gods and an innocent dolphin has also been killed, bearing the weight of my curse.'

As he listened, the tohunga watched Ruru with his wise, dark eyes.

'You must be punished for the wrong you have done; the

84

terrible madness of murder must never touch you again. The world must be protected from you.'

Ruru was speechless and afraid. He cowered as he waited for the tohunga's decree.

The tohunga, performing the rituals of makutu, his special magic powers, drew from the body of Ruru, the very soul.

'May your wairua now replace the once living spirit of that dolphin,' he chanted. 'And may it stay there for as long as you are a threat to those around you. In your new life you shall give welcome to the canoes that reach the entrance of the Pass along the Sound.'

And so, the soul of Ruru, embodied by the dolphin, swam the waters of the coast, far from the villages and treacherous cliffs, escorting each vessel that entered his new territory.

The sight of the dolphin became famous and in time, Ruru the man-soul acquired the new name of Pelorus Jack, the dolphin. But the soul, ever restless, sought some kind of release. Each year he returned to the tohunga and begged for his former existence. And each year the tohunga refused, saying it was his duty to preserve peace.

Back to the waves went Ruru, disappointed yet never completely resigned. He bounded and leapt and hailed the wood canoes, hoping they might help him, that they would know who he really was. But only the tohunga knew the true identity of Pelorus Jack.

One year, as he reached the shore again and made his way to his village, he felt a strong sense of foreboding; it made him shiver. His soul, his man-soul, rippled with stifled anger. The tohunga was dead. The new holy-man did not recognize Ruru, nor could he help when he heard his story.

'I beg you to put an end to my lonely torture,' said Ruru. 'They wave and they greet me; they see me there in the water, leaping ahead, guiding them on their way. But I have no one, no friend, no companion, only the touch of the boats; a hard, unfriendly bruise.'

There was nothing the new tohunga could do; it was

prohibited for one tohunga to disclose his particular accomp-
lishments to another.

So Pelorus Jack guided the small canoes and the men with
their paddles that dashed the waves and foam. Some thought
his great energy, the way he jumped in the air then nosed the
level blue again, was an invitation to sport and play. They
raced towards the Pass then left him, quite alone.

Time went on. The Pakeha, the white-man, began to
arrive in the region where Pelorus Jack continued his peaceful
mission. And the soul of Ruru grew quiet. He saw the once
familiar Maori, his own race, lessen in number. The sheltered
bays soon boasted large towns, and the remembrance of his
village saddened Ruru, entrapped as he was inside the dolphin
body. It seemed there could be no greater loneliness than this.
He wondered when his misery would end.

And then it was discovered that Pelorus Jack had
vanished. The time was 1916. Far across the world men
fought each other and millions of lives were lost. In the southern seas huge ships of iron passed by Pelorus Sound.

Could it be that the dolphin was not seen by the metal
monsters and so its work became useless? Or had the first
tohunga seen into the future and found there a time when the
man-soul's anger might meet a greater and more powerful
enemy? Who can tell?

12

Fairest of
All Others

A BOX; it was a box and it was floating on the
incoming tide. Each wave that swelled and burst upon the
shore brought it nearer until at last its base touched the sand
and it remained there, the tide turning on its outward flow.

Coming down the heather-decked path from the village,
an elderly fisherman paused to survey the outline of the cove.
He always stopped there. He sat on the top of the flight of
wooden steps that he and his friends had built, long ago, and
he drew a few sharp breaths, summoning up more strength for
the final descent to the beach. But this day his rest was
prolonged. His eyes were fixed to the object that stood just
short of the margin of pale grey shingle.

'Now what has the sea brought me today?' he wondered.

Usually, before preparing his boat with lines and bait, he
would amble round the bare expanse of sand, his aged back
bent, his tired eyes scanning each space between rock and
stone. Sometimes he found a perfectly shaped shell, unbroken
by its rough sea-journey or he'd reach for a clouded green
bottle, excited for a few seconds in case it contained a piece of
paper, a message written in some strange, foreign hand. Odd
twists of rope, a clump of slippery seaweed whose brown
shoots straggled flat green tendrils, a rusting piece of metal

scrap: all these things he'd scrutinize with interest before he began his work.

When he saw the box, seemingly intact, he could only stare. His mind raced on thoughts of smuggled goods; brandy, ammunition, perhaps even gold. He was unsure whether he dared go down to inspect it, but at last, on reaching the beach, he moved one sandalled foot before the other, slowly, until he was within a yard of where the box lay.

He stared for a full four minutes. Then he reached out his hand, but before his frail old fingers had touched the wooden casket, he jumped with fright.

The unmistakable sound of a baby's cry came from inside the box.

'Good heavens! What kind of treasure is this?'

With his fishing knife, he prized open the nailed lid and sure enough, lying quite secure and warm in a stretch of woollen cloth was a baby girl. He cupped his hands and took her to his chest, patting her round head to silence her tears. Then he looked up to the cliff-top and wondered how he'd manage to climb all those steps again so soon. But home he had to take her.

When his wife saw him walking over the back field towards their cottage, she could not understand why he had returned.

'Perhaps the chill winds have finally reached his bones. I always knew there'd come a day when the sea made him welcome no longer. Ah, but it is a shame; for what shall I do with him all day long, he in his eighty-first year and myself a mere seventy-three? Why – see how he is bent, clutching his hands to his breast . . . .'

When she lifted the latch and had opened the back door, she saw he carried the child.

They agreed to keep her and bring her up themselves, old though they were. They had never had any children and they felt, since the sea had been their livelihood, it was only right that they should claim what the sea had brought them.

The people of the village visited the old pair and delighted in seeing their tiny girl. No one doubted that they should keep her. The couple had only one regret: that their poverty would provide little for the child when they should die.

One day, having heard of the extraordinary circumstances by which the baby had reached the village, the local squire's son arrived at the old fisherman's door.

'Yes, I'd be terribly grateful if you'd let me see the baby,' he said, taking off his hat as he walked into their parlour. There was something about his manner they could not refuse and the sight of his grand clothes made them silent.

'As a matter of fact,' the squire's son went on, 'I'm rather good at telling fortunes. Would you let me have a go at hers?'

'Yes – oh yes, sir, if it pleases,' said the old lady.

The squire's son placed the baby's crib (that same wooden box now lined with the prettiest, fresh linen) upon the table and proceeded to take from his jacket pocket a deck of cards, a compass and a scroll of parchment.

'Got a cup of tea?' he asked.

'Oh yes sir, do you take milk with it?'

'No, no. I mean an empty cup, one that you've used.'

'Oh I see sir,' said the old lady, as she bustled to her scullery and reappeared with the cup she'd used not long before his arrival.

'Fine, fine,' said the squire's son and he began to lay the cards upon the tablecloth.

The fisherman and his wife stood by and watched as he examined the tea-leaves that lined the cup, moved the compass round and round and turned up each card.

'Mmmmm,' he mumbled. 'A beauty I see, and still more cups and saucers, plates, knives and food. . . . '

The old couple looked at each other, bewildered. Then they noticed that the squire's son was frowning.

'No, no – it cannot be. . . . '

'What?' they asked, now becoming concerned.

'I must try this one again.'

He turned the compass round, shuffled the cards, squinted at the tea-leaves and read the scroll of paper. Then suddenly he stood up from the table.

'I want to make you an offer,' he announced, staring the fisherman and his wife in their faces, almost simultaneously.

'What's that?' they asked.

'I should like to buy this child. You know you cannot provide for her, nor leave her any wealth when you are gone. With my help she could grow to be a lady and need have no fear of ever being poor.'

They looked at one another, unsure of what to say. So the squire's son went on.

'I'll give you two hundred pounds if you let me take her now.'

For the old fisherman and his wife, two hundred pounds was a large sum of money. However, it grieved them to part with the baby; they loved her dearly. But at last, thinking of her welfare, they agreed to let her go.

'Very well,' the fisherman declared. 'But take her quickly before we break our hearts in saying goodbye. And may we ask for one more thing?'

'What's that?' said the squire's son hurriedly.

'That you leave us the box in which she came to us. For it was the best piece of treasure I ever came across.'

The squire's son left their cottage as quick as lightning. With the baby securely tied to him by the bright, white cravat he wore around his neck, he rode his horse at speed and soon reached the stables of the manor where he lived. He saw his groom at work and commanded him:

'Make me a box, about eighteen inches long, twelve across and twelve inches deep.'

'Yes, sir,' said the groom, recognizing the urgency of his master's request without seeing what he held in his arms.

As he waited in the stable-yard, the squire's son paced about, talking to himself.

'Marry me indeed! Why, this child was washed up on the shore; who knows where she has come from? To marry me would be an insult. And yet twice the cards and the leaves and compass told me it was true. She must not marry me.'

When the new box was ready, the squire's son rode away with it and the baby girl, over to the cliff-tops. Down the wooden steps he went, and before he placed her in the box he drew out a knife from his belt. Holding her head in one hand, he slashed a cross on her cheek. Without waiting to hear her cries, he nailed her in the box and waded out to sea until he saw the waves were strong enough to carry her with them. He left the box and the child to fate.

The old fisherman, despite his wife's fears, was not too infirm to continue with his daily walk across the sands before venturing out to catch fish. Some days after they had sold their child to the squire's son, he returned to the top of the wooden steps and sighed as he watched the waves. Then he blinked. He rubbed his eyes and he blinked again.

'Can it be true, or is my vision playing the tricks of old age upon me?'

For there, as if it were an exact repetition of what had taken place earlier, he saw a box washed up on the shore, just below the shingle.

Without hesitating, he raced to the spot, as fast as his legs would carry him and quickly opened the box.

'Our little girl – it is our little girl, but oh – what terrible mark is that upon your face?'

He held the baby close in case she stirred and gladly he took her home again. His wife, like him, was overjoyed to see her and alarmed by the sight of her wound.

'We must make sure that, while we live, she shall never leave our sight,' they both agreed.

So, as the years passed, the baby grew to love and care for her old parents. By the time she was seventeen years old, she managed all the household chores herself. To pass the hours of leisure, she would walk outside alone, but she never wandered further than the sea-shore. When her old father asked her to tell him what she found there, she willingly described each shell, each patterned stone, each starfish that she'd seen. Listening to her, he was able to remember how it had been when he too had roamed the sands.

In time the old fisherman and his wife died, and when the girl found she had no one else to cook and care for but herself and no money left from her parents' store of coins, she let it be known that she sought some kind of work. As they asked here and there on her behalf, the people of the village couldn't help describing the girl herself; not only was she capable and hard-working, she was also the most beautiful girl in the neighbourhood.

'Oh yes, an' it is despite that dreadful cross on 'er face. For she is lovely as a spring mornin' and 'er soul's as fresh as well,' they said.

It just so happened that up at the manor house, the kitchens had fallen into a state of chaos. The chief cook was ill and few of the remaining staff could make head or tail of the squire's handwriting. Besides, without anyone to give them orders, they didn't know which finger to put in what pie next. The squire was furious and charged his son to go and find a replacement cook.

Into the village rode the squire's son; the people bowed and bobbed their heads as they saw him. His first call was at the inn, then the baker's and the blacksmith's and the draper's shop. In each place he was told of the lovely girl, now living alone in that same cottage he had visited, once, years ago.

Without further inquiry the squire's son made straight for the cliff-top cottage and hammered on the door, peeping at the same time through the curtains, in case he could gain an early glimpse of the beauty he had heard so much about.

She opened the door to him and curtsied. He gasped with wonder, but his expression changed in an instant. Though her skin was the colour of rosebuds and her dark eyes showed the

93

light of her mild soul, his admiration ceased when he saw the scar on her cheek.

She looked down, ashamed, and put her hand across the scar.

'I see you stare at the mark on my face, sir. It has been with me all my life.'

'All your life indeed. No matter about your face. I came to ask you to cook for me. I hear you are seeking work. Come now, and I shall show you our kitchens where no one shall see you. I shall reward you fairly.'

He seemed in a hurry, so the girl tidied herself quickly and followed him outside. But as he was striding towards the wooden steps that led down to the beach, she called out to him.

'Oh no, sir. That way leads only to the sea. There's nothing there but – '

'I know. Be quiet. Follow me.'

She did as she was told though she was puzzled he should lead her there. When she reached the sand she stared out at the dappled afternoon sun that bounced across the water. She turned to see where the squire's son was taking her and soon she found she was falling to her knees in a half-swoon. For he had drawn his sword and was about to strike her.

'Oh sir, what reason have you for this?' she pleaded.

'I will not say. Let it suffice that I cannot let you live.'

'Not live? And who are you to take away a life?' she asked, rising to her feet again.

'I – I am – '

'Yes? Who are you? And who am I? Only two people facing each other. It is not for one of us to deal the other's fate.'

As she talked, he let his sword fall. There was something so compelling in the way she spoke and the keen, long look with which she faced him, that he found he had to listen to her.

'Look at the tide,' she said, pointing to the sea behind them. 'Is there any man who could stop or push or pull that

power, just because he wishes it? No. Our lives, like the ebb
and flow of the water, must go the way they will.'

He was by now quite mesmerized by her speech, but to
save his pride he could not let her go so easily.

'Very well. I shall spare you. But I warn you, if ever I see
you again, then I shall kill you.'

Her eyes remained fixed on his own; she neither smiled nor
sighed. For a moment he did not know what to do; her beauty
and her gentle look stunned him completely.

'Unless,' he stammered, 'unless you show me this ring.'

He pulled off a large, gold signet-ring from his little finger.
She was about to take it from him when he turned and tossed it
far out into the sea. Then he left her, ran up the wooden steps
and out of sight. The girl remained staring out at the wide,
deep ocean.

In time, thanks to the continued effort of all her friends in the
village, the girl was informed that a grand and noble lady
required a young cook at her hunting lodge. This house, the
girl found out, was happily situated a good many miles from
the village and the manor and the squire's son. She accepted
the post with gladness when it was offered her.

Working in the kitchens, though her hands became rough
and raw, and her back ached and her eyes smarted with the
cooking fumes, the girl never lost her beauty.

When they had grown to know and love her, the other
people working there – the butlers and the housemaids, the
stablehands and grooms – they chatted and they puzzled and
occasionally inquired about her scar.

'I don't know how it happened. I've had it all my life.'

Even the grand lady, hearing of the girl who cooked in her
kitchens, asked to see her.

'Yes, it is true. You are quite lovely. Why, you should be
called Fairest of all Others, for there is no one fairer than you.'

And so the fame of her beauty spread across the neighbourhood. It reached the bustling town and it climbed the highest

hill. It blew through the valley and back to the sea. Everyone knew of Fairest of all Others, though few had seen her. A fishmonger, thrilled at the opportunity of meeting the lovely girl, stayed in the kitchens of the lodge for a full hour and a half. He sat astride a chair, his arms across its back, his head on his arms and he stared at her. She didn't complain, but chatted pleasantly as she prepared the fish.

'An' why is it you've not got yourself a husband?' asked the fishmonger.

'I'll not go in search of one,' she said.

'No, but there's surely somethin' wrong with your bein' here like this. Why, you have the charm and the grace of a true lady. You could have any man you choose.'

'I'll not choose nor be chosen. 'Tis best to leave things to the way they must be.'

The fishmonger left, shaking his head, not quite understanding what she had said. She smiled as she saw him go and continued with her work. But as she sliced the fish he had brought, she noticed something hard, like a stone, in one of them. She cut and she scraped and she washed out the body and there she found a ring, that same signet-ring that the squire's son had cast into the sea. Smiling again, she popped it in her apron pocket.

There was a banquet at the lodge that night. The chandeliers blazed their light across the lawn from the tall windows. The polished floors gleamed like mirrors. Flowers filled every room with fragrance. As the carriages arrived, the household staff stared from their secret hiding-places. The feast was announced and a bustle of agitation began to stir in the kitchens.

'Now let us not be anxious and we shall all get by,' said the girl. It had been decided that, because of her beauty and her natural grace, she should be the one to carry the silver dish into the banquet hall.

Having arranged the last slice of lemon across the neat rows of fish, she carefully made her way up the stairs. When she entered the large room the faces turned, the whispers rose.

'Fairest of all Others she is called. And so it is true, despite the cross upon her cheek.'

But there was one guest who was not so pleased: the squire's son. He stood at the table, his face as black as thunder. Then he roared, silencing the other guests:

'I never thought I'd live to see you mock me this way!'

'Mock you?' replied the girl, still carrying the dish. She moved forward and placed it before him, touching the fish with the long, marked side, the one that had carried his ring. 'You only ridicule yourself. If you wish to talk to me, come and leave these people to their meal.'

She curtsied to her mistress and left the hall. The squire's son, remembering how he had felt the last time he had heard her speak, stood still for a moment. Then he ran after her.

As soon as he found her he drew his sword, but he noticed that she smiled and her soft eyes looked up at him without a trace of fear.

'I said I would kill you – I shall,' he cried, dismayed by her great calm.

'You shall not. For I have the ring that you cast to the seas. I have our fate in my pocket.'

She lifted the ring before his eyes and he stared at it in disbelief.

Then he knelt at her feet in submission.

'The sea has brought you to me; the sea will not let us part,' he said, as he felt her forgiving hand upon his shoulder.

13

The Merrow and
the Soul Cages

THERE was a fisherman, Jack Docherty was his
name, who lived with his wife Biddy in a small cottage near
the sea. Though all his family had earned their living quite
peaceably by fishing, Jack remembered the tales of his grand-
father in particular. It was his grandfather who had once
known a merrow.

The female merrows are beautiful; they dance among the
waves and comb their hair in the heat of the summer sun, not
unlike mermaids of whom we know so much. The male merrows however, are beastly-looking creatures; their bodies and
their hair and their teeth are livid green; their eyes like pigs'
eyes are on either side of long, red noses and they have short,
scaly arms.

Jack longed to see a merrow. Each day he went along the
shore and often quite far out to sea in search of one. It was not
until his boat was cruising among the jutting rocks nearby that
Jack's longing was quite unexpectedly satisfied. A merrow was
sitting on the hard, dark surface of a single, glistening rock. He
held in his hand a red, pointed hat. At times he put on the hat
and dived into the lapping waves. Jack could hardly contain
his excitement, but he didn't dare approach the merrow.

Back at home he spent a sleepless night wondering how his
grandfather had ever come to be on friendly terms with such a

clumsy and peculiar creature. He would never know unless he too attempted to be friends. The next day, though a storm raged and the sea and sky were whipped and tossed by wind, Jack returned to the rock and there he found the merrow, the same one surely, playing in the waves quite unconcerned. To his surprise the merrow, on seeing him, hailed him.

'Hallo there, Docherty! Come over here!'

Jack steered towards the rock, speechless.

'Yes, I know you, though I must say I knew your grand-father better. Loved his drink, didn't he? And so do I, so do I,' said the merrow.

'Drink? You drink?' asked Jack, finding his voice at last. 'Where do you get yours from, out here?'

'Where?' replied the merrow. 'And where do you, Jack? What about those casks that are swept up on the shore, eh? Why, I've a cellar full of the stuff at home.'

'Home? Where is your home?'

'Come back tomorrow. I'll show you. Better still, you shall dine with me.'

Jack could hardly wait until the next day and the next time he could see the merrow. When the evening light began to disappear, leaving a pink tinge across the horizon, Jack was soon back at the rock where he saw the merrow, this time holding two red hats.

'Now put this on,' said the merrow, offering Jack one of the hats and placing it on his head very carefully. 'Hold on to my tail and keep your eyes open. Away we go!'

Jack did as he was told, and when they had dived and reached the bottom of the sea, he was relieved to find a stretch of dry land. He could breath and see quite easily and above him the sea with its fishes seemed like the sky and all its stars. Jack followed the merrow into his home and watched him prepare a splendid meal which he placed, together with sever-al bottles and a pair of tankards, upon his wooden table. They drank and they drank and they sang many a song that grand-father Docherty had known in his day.

'Oh yes, we had a rare old time he and I,' said the merrow.
'By the way Jack, my name is Coomara. Shall I show you my
house?'

Jack nodded and was led from one room to the next until he
came to the merrow's store of curiosities. A row of what
appeared to be old lobster pots caught his attention. They
didn't seem very precious to him. He asked Coomara why he
kept them.

'Those are the soul cages,' Coomara replied.

'Soul cages? But fish don't have souls.'

'Certainly they don't. Here I keep the souls of sailors.
When a storm blows above I cast the cages upon the sea and
the sand and I catch them, the sailors' souls, and I bring them
down here to keep warm.'

Jack felt peculiar. He thought it might be time to leave,
what with the drink and the knowledge he now possessed. He
made an excuse.

'All right then. It's been good having you, Jack Docherty.
If you want to come back just pop a stone in the water near the
rock and I'll bring you up a hat. Oh – you'll need one now – but
it has to be the other way round for the return journey.'

Jack was unsure of his ability to swim without the merrow.
He spied a large cod not far overhead. He could hold on to the
cod's tail. But no sooner had the red hat touched the water,
than Jack was bounding through the waves and had landed
back on the rock once more.

That night, he couldn't help remembering the line of cages
and the captured souls of many hapless sailors who had
drowned so near the merrow's home. Should he tell Biddy?
Perhaps it was best if he told the priest; this sort of thing was
more in his line. But word might get round that he was closely
acquainted with a merrow and others might not understand
that they were amiable creatures, despite their looks. Besides,
Coomara wasn't a bad sort at all. No one would believe you
could sit and laugh and drink – the drink – that was it. That's
what his grandfather had loved; that's what Coomara loved. If

he returned and invited Coomara to drink with him here, at the cottage, and made him so drunk he couldn't move, then he could go back himself, and set the souls free.

At last, a week later, Jack went back to the rock, threw a stone in the water and summoned Coomara to his side.

'I think it is only fair that you should be my guest tonight, Coomara,' he said, and he saw the green teeth flash beneath the merrow's smile as he accepted.

There was, however, one obstacle in the way of his plan's success; Biddy. She would surely faint at the idea of a merrow at her kitchen table. Thinking, he went home.

'Now Bid,' he sighed, 'I've a fear that the calm weather'll not be here for long. We must pray for the souls of men who have drowned and those in danger of drownin'.'

'Oh yes, Jack. Heaven forbid!' she replied, fearfully.

'Myself included, Biddy dear. Perhaps you should pay a short visit to the church for I have an odd feeling deep inside my bones.'

'Don't say so, Jack. If it's prayin' will help, I'll be off right away.'

With the house free for entertaining, Jack busied himself and awaited his guest.

The two friends ate and they drank and they sang, but the more they drank, the more Jack became dizzy. There was no cool water above his head now. He saw the merrow laughing, complaining quite jokingly, that he was not like his grandfather. When the time for Biddy's return drew near, Jack had to hurry Coomara away as he puzzled the explanations he would give her for the turmoil and the mess in the kitchen. It was best to tell her the truth. He heard her steps at the garden gate and he went out to greet her.

He told her of his first meeting with Coomara, of his trip to his home and of the sailors' souls, trapped in cages below the sea.

'Oh dear, oh dear, oh my!' exclaimed Biddy. 'You must free them Jack, those souls of drowned sailors.'

Together they thought and they hummed and they ha'd until they struck on the best plan. The merrow was a homely creature, fond of company and not at all offensive. He was naturally very glad to have found a friend again, the grandson of his former friend. They would invite him once more, but this time they would give him that home-made brandy – potcheen – brewed by Biddy's brother, and the strongest liquor in the land. The merrow could never have tasted it.

Coomara was glad to return so soon to Jack's cottage. He drank and he laughed and he sang and he drank, but unlike Jack (whose potcheen had been cautiously watered down) he fell across his arms, slumped at the kitchen table and was soon snoring, fast asleep.

Jack leapt up and ran out into the cold. He held Coomara's hat beneath his arm and dived through the sea to the merrow regions of the deep. He ran to the room of curiosities and there he saw the line of cages. Quickly, he reached towards the first and turned it on its side. He wasn't sure, but he thought he heard a faint and gentle sigh as a pale, glimmering light rose up and disappeared into the sea. Each time, at each cage, the flicker ascended and at last Jack stepped back and stared. They all looked just as he had seen them a minute or two earlier. Coomara would not be able to tell the difference.

Jack often entertained the merrow to a meal and a glass or two of potcheen. And each time, when a storm had raged or a sailing-ship ran aground, Jack crept out, went down to the sea and tipped up the soul cages one by one. He was always back at the kitchen table before Coomara awoke.

One day, when he stood upon the rock and had dropped the stone into the water, Jack waited longer than usual. He expected to see the familiar green and hairy hand reach out, then the face and the short, scaly body. Nothing happened. Coomara couldn't be dead; he was only several hundred years old and still a youngster.

Perhaps he had moved to another part of the sea. But without the red hat, Jack was never to know.

14

Duke Magnus
and the Mermaid

A TALE has often been told of noble Duke Magnus, the youngest son of the royal Vasa family of Småland. Each morning, when the sun was up and before he set about his daily duties, he would stand at the uppermost window of his castle and look out on the country that stretched from the hills to the coast. It always pleased him to do this; he could collect his thoughts together as he surveyed his kinsmen's territory.

It happened that one such morning, as he breathed deeply the fresh salt air, he noticed how the tide swelled and rushed by at a most unusual pace. He remained standing, watching. Then he heard a voice.

'Duke Magnus, Duke Magnus . . . .'

It was a woman's voice and as sweet and pure as the strains of a viola or, as it went on calling his name, as soft and enticing as the liquid notes of a harp. He leaned over the narrow, stone window-ledge to see who was there and immediately his eyes fell upon a rock set in the middle of the estuary. Clinging to its side was the loveliest woman he had ever seen.

>*'Duke Magnus, Duke Magnus, plight thee to*
>*me . . . .'*

she called, or was she singing he wondered, as he saw the fair
coils of her hair cluster and fall into the water at her waist.

>*'Say me not nay, but yes, yes,'*

she murmured as he blinked in disbelief.

At last he was able to speak: 'Who are you? What do you
want of me?'

She fingered the rock playfully then swung round to face
him as he stared.

>*'O, to you I will give a travelling ship,*
>*The best that a knight would guide;*
>*A ship that will sail on water and land*
>*And over the fields so wide . . . .'*

The Duke listened and, from the height where he stood, he
began to feel dizzy. The distant hills, the meadows and the
swirling ripples of water seemed to blur in the dazzling sunshine as he heard her voice sing on:

>*'So say me not nay, but yes, yes.*
>*For I will give you a fearless horse,*
>*The best that a knight would ride;*
>*A horse that will move on water and land*
>*And 'cross the seas so wide . . . .'*

He saw the drawbridge that spanned the narrow moat of
his castle. He almost leapt from the window. But as he
touched the steel edge of the sword at his side, he stopped still
and answered:

'I serve the king and my native land. There is no woman
shall sway me from my first allegiance. Besides, how should I

find peace, married to one such as you, whoever, whatever you are?'

He stood upright, his hands firm upon the cold, castle stone.

'*Say me not nay, but yes, yes,*'

came the voice and in an instant the lovely woman had swerved and dived into the water out of sight.

For a long while Duke Magnus remained watching until he decided he must have been day-dreaming. Or perhaps the responsibilities of his household, the various courts he had to arrange with his brothers and dependants, were weighing on his mind and he needed rest.

That night he summoned his page earlier than usual. He was soon clothed in his night-gown, a candle by his large, curtained bed, ready to sleep. But sleep did not come to Duke Magnus. Though he closed his eyes, he saw before him the vision of the lovely woman, her long hair as bright as the sunlight that moved in the fast flowing water. He tossed and he turned and as he groaned he could hear her voice calling to him as it had done the morning before.

When his page arrived with fruit to eat and water to wake him fully, Duke Magnus was already sitting up. As soon as he was dressed he returned to the small tower at the top of the castle. This time he stood back and eyed the narrow window with a mixture of fear and longing. Hardly moving a single muscle, he waited and listened to the silence of the new day. He was about to turn and leave when the voice, that same voice that had teased him for many hours, sung its way through the open space to strike his heart with trouble.

'*Duke Magnus, Duke Magnus, plight thee to me.*
Say me not nay, but yes, yes.'

He ran forward, determined to shout aloud, to send her

away with the threat of his sword and shield. But when he saw her, now sitting on the rock, her fair skin turning to shining, green scales at her waist, he gasped and could say nothing.

> *'O, to you I will give such stores of gold*
> *That will last till your life endure.*
> *And pearls and gems from ages old,*
> *Unscath'd, untouched, ever pure.*
> *So say me not nay, but yes, yes.'*

As she called she held out her arms to him and beckoned. The wind from the sea blew through the valley and lifted her hair from her face. The Duke called out, 'Yes, yes – gladly would I plight me to thee!' Immediately he felt his hands tremble and loosen their hold as his shield and sword fell to the floor with a resounding clamour that deafened his ears to her ceaseless call. Turning sharply to retrieve them, he resolved to be firm. He raised his sword and pointed it towards her.

'I am of royal blood and Christian faith. I cannot let you love me. And you – why you live in the flood, on the tides, in the sea. You are nothing but a vile sea-troll!'

The waters rose around her, foaming at the rock as if in anger. But she, quite calmly, placed her hands in her scaly green lap and tossed back her hair.

> *'Duke Magnus, Duke Magnus, think you well*
> *And answer me not so haughtily.*
> *For to you and your kin*
> *Will come madness therein,*
> *From now till eternity.'*

The noble Duke never saw her again though he returned to the window every day. It is said that whenever he, or any of his descendants, looked out on the lands of their family, they saw not the meadows leading down from the hills to the sea, but sights so terrible, only madmen could describe them.

15

The Sea Captain
and the Serpent

A MAN was often to be seen walking along the Spanish coast, his eyes downcast as his feet toyed with the sand, his hands in his pockets. Mahistruba was his name; he was once a sea-captain, but since losing his ship he had become poor and the livelihood he once so loved was also lost to him. It could be said that in wandering like that, with the sea so near, yet without the means to sail there, he was asking to be made unhappy. The main reason for his chosen solitude was that he wanted to avoid his wife and his daughter who spent their days working hard, keeping the family together. He had his pride.

Each day as he walked, Mahistruba met a serpent that lay coiled in the sand dunes until, on seeing him arrive, it slid forward to greet him. Mahistruba was never afraid of the serpent, in fact he became quite fond of it, appreciating its apparent freedom.

'God has given you life; then live on, O serpent,' said Mahistruba.

The serpent recognized Mahistruba's plight.

'I see how your luck has changed. I see how you mourn the loss of your working days, how you long to be back on the seas again, how empty and sad the hours must be for you. You have been kind to me where others might have been frightened and turned away. If you will trust me, I can help you.'

The serpent advised Mahistruba to have a ship built, to pay the builders double the price they asked for and to find twelve strong sailors for the crew.

'I will provide you with money,' ended the serpent.

Mahistruba felt his courage return as he saw the progress of a fine ship in the builder's yard. From where he lived he could hear the hammering of nails in wood and with each crack that sounded, he knew he was closer to being back on the seas again. He pinned up a notice asking for men of good health and experience to contact him, and soon he had his crew of twelve who welcomed the wages that were offered them and looked forward to their journey.

'But where are we going?' Mahistruba asked the serpent, when all that was needed was a third coat of paint on the ship.

'I shall tell you as we go along.'

'You?'

'Yes, I. I want you to find one more thing; a deep chest into which I may creep and remain hidden. Your sailors, unlike you, may be alarmed by my presence.'

So it came about that on the day of sailing, when the townsfolk came from their houses and the wife and daughter of Mahistruba wept with a mixture of sadness and relief, the serpent coiled itself inside the chest and was taken on board the ship. Under the careful supervision of Mahistruba, it was placed safely in the corner of his cabin.

They sailed eastwards; the sun accompanied them, adding to their pleasure. When he had finished his dinner, Mahistruba took the serpent from the chest and gladly walked round his cabin as it lay across his shoulders.

'Tell me where are we bound,' he said.

'In time, in time. But first I must say that this joyous venture is to have its hazards. Tonight there will be a great storm. During the storm a bird will fly above us. I want you to find among the crew an expert marksman who will shoot the bird when it is overhead.'

'I will. But I am intrigued to know what this means.'

'Time, time. I will tell you in time.'

Up on the deck the crew were surprised to be called at such a late hour, just as they looked forward to their hard-earned sleep. Mahistruba lined them up and asked which one considered he was a good shot with the rifle. There was a pause. Then one man stepped forward.

'I can shoot a swallow in flight. I've never missed yet,' he said.

'Very well; you will do nicely.'

Mahistruba told the serpent a man had been chosen.

'Good. Then give him some of the magic potion that is in a bottle in the chest.'

The man was tied to the mast; the storm was already whipping up and by the time the waves were raging, sending shoots of dazzling spray over the deck and the ship rolled from side to side, Mahistruba and his crew were a little afraid. At last a wild cry was heard and in the pale light of the moon the broad wings of a dark bird were seen black against the scudding clouds.

The marksman aimed and fired and the bird fell to the deck, dead.

Mahistruba told the serpent that all he had predicted had taken place and the bird was now cast into the sea.

'Very good. Now I shall tell you of what we shall do next, for I know we are nearing the land,' said the serpent. 'Soon we shall reach a port, a pleasant place where the houses are of pastel shades and the sun beats down upon their stone almost every day of the year. We are to stop there. Round about the town are many hills. I want you to find the man who can run the fastest of all of us.'

The next day Mahistruba lined up his crew on the deck. He asked which man considered himself a fit and fast runner. One of the twelve stepped forward.

'I can catch a hare as it races across the fields,' he said.

'Very well; you will do nicely.'

The serpent was pleased to hear of this and proceeded to deliver to Mahistruba further instructions.

'He must run to a cottage on the southern hill where he will find an old woman; a woman who will make him most unwelcome. He will need to visit her three times and on each occasion, though he will be much weakened, he must take from her home some certain objects.'

They were glad to see the port; its colours and sunny appearance warmed their hearts. As soon as the ship had docked the runner was sent on his errand. He ran and he ran and he ran. He arrived at the cottage and knocked on the door which soon was opened an inch or two, hardly at all, but enough for him to see an old, gnarled face, peering at him, staring.

'I'm so very tired. I've walked so far. I beg you for a drink,' he said, gasping.

'Certainly not,' replied the old woman, making to slam the door, but he held it ajar with the palm of his hand.

'Please – I won't stay long.'

'You'd better not,' she snapped as she reluctantly let him in.

No sooner had she done this, and disappeared into her kitchen, than he searched her front room and saw, on the window-sill, the small, steel slab he knew he had to take. He slipped it into his pocket. She thrust the glass of water into his hand and he gladly left, as soon as he had gulped it down.

He began to run but soon he heard a screeching behind him; it was the old woman, her hands waving wildly above her, shouting, following him. He guessed she had discovered her loss. He was quite surprised to find she ran as fast as he did, faster even, and when her fingers touched him he screamed. With her long, sharp nails she tore the skin from his back, then returned laughing.

The runner reached the ship exhausted.

'Give him some magic balm I have in the chest,' said the serpent on hearing all that had happened.

The ointment's power began to heal the man's almost fleshless back immediately. He slept well; a calm and dreamless sleep. And when he woke the next day he hardly feared returning to the cottage. It was as if he'd almost forgotten.

Arriving at the old woman's door he received the same welcome as the day before.

'But I've been shipwrecked. I need just a piece of coal to help me light a fire,' he said.

Again she let him in only because of his persistence. When she was out of the front room he spied upon a shelf the flint he was to take away with him. He slipped it into his pocket and hoped the coal that she gave him would fit in also.

As he ran from her garden gate he could hear her shout with vexation behind him. And try as hard as he might, he could not escape her chase. She tore the skin from his back, his neck and shoulders, all at once.

'The magic balm, the magic balm will save him,' said the serpent on hearing Mahistruba's news. Mahistruba was now rather distressed that a member of his crew should be suffering so.

'When will I know what all this means?' he asked.

'In time, in time. It will not be long now.'

Through the night, the runner slept peacefully and was quite prepared to visit the house of the old woman once again. He hadn't remembered a thing.

The old woman snarled as she saw him at the door.

'Go away. I've had visitors enough these past two days and I don't want more!' she said.

'It's two days since I've eaten,' said the runner, 'and all I ask is a piece of bread.'

As she went to the kitchen to fetch it, he saw the tinder box he knew he had to find, upon the mantelpiece. He fled from the cottage as soon as it was in his pocket, and only minutes later he heard her yell behind him. With her nimble, bony hands she

ripped the skin from his neck, his shoulders, his legs and down to his heels. Instead of turning back, she stood there screaming to the sky, shaking her fists about her. The runner, despite his agony, couldn't help but listen and watch.

'So be it! I'm done for now! The three are gone; the spell will soon be over!' she cried.

To his astonishment, as she finished her last exclamation she disappeared entirely, as if into the thin, sunny air, there on the wide, green hilltop.

When the runner reached the ship, moaning with pain, Mahistruba marched straight into his cabin, thrust open the chest, and with a note of anger he himself was astonished to find, he demanded an explanation from the serpent.

'Certainly – very soon now. Tomorrow I want you to sound seven cannons across the bay. This will rouse the King from his palace.'

'But cannon-fire is banned from this country. I will be arrested.'

'Do as I say; all will be well.'

Before the seven cannons had rung across the hills, the police of that port were down in the docks and aboard the ship where they took hold of Mahistruba and escorted him to their prison.

Lonely, and decidedly confused, Mahistruba begged the chance to talk to someone about his state; the journey he had taken and the advice of the serpent.

'If I could see the King I feel sure he'd understand,' he said.

Surprisingly, the King did come to see Mahistruba. He had heard about the gentle sea-captain who was so unlike the vagrants and other ruffians there.

'Well now,' said the King on entering his cell. 'There has to be a good reason behind all this. Did you know that cannon has been prohibited here ever since the disappearance of my son, seven years ago?'

'No, no, your Majesty. I'm sure I wouldn't have done

anything to displease you were it not for the trust I have in a strange sea-serpent who has long been my friend.'

The King heard a full account of all that had happened from Mahistruba's first meeting with the serpent until his arrival in prison. He decided to board the ship to see the serpent for himself. Mahistruba was allowed to accompany him.

On entering the cabin Mahistruba pointed to the chest in the corner.

'There – the serpent lies within that chest. You are the first person, besides myself, to know this, your Majesty.'

The King moved forward and opened the chest boldly. The serpent wriggled, crept over the wooden side and on reaching the floor it cried out, 'My father!' and instantly it turned into a person, a young man, a prince.

Tears came to the eyes of the King as the once-serpent Prince explained his story to him, Mahistruba and all the crew who were immediately summoned.

'A spell was cast upon me, long ago, when I chanced to wander over these hills. An old woman, a witch indeed, envied me my royal state and turned me into a serpent, thinking that creature a suitably frightening one. She said no man lived who was kind enough to offer friendship to a serpent. She believed that were I cast upon a distant shore, I should soon be killed. But she was wrong. A friend did come to help me.'

The King immediately ordered the chains from Mahistruba's hands to be unlocked. The Prince went on:

'His kind words were the hope I lived by. And more than this, I understood his sadness, his longing for the seas. In the same way I too had loved to roam our hills though I met with misfortune there. Ill-luck can find us anywhere, be we prince or sailor. But fortune also smiles upon us. The witch's servant, a wild night-bird, was shot down not long after we left. The spell she cast was broken when her three favourite treasures were taken from her house; only I knew what they were. And so she was destroyed, thanks to this man's trust.'

114

The cannons on all the ships in the port sounded out across the green hills: the church bells pealed. The whole town cheered the return of their lost Prince.

In the royal court, each member of the crew was given gold coins, enough to last all their lives. In addition, the marksman received a rifle of gold studded with gems, that fired diamond bullets. And the runner welcomed his golden shoes with their laces of silver thread. They matched exactly the jacket that was lined across the back with the strongest metal of the land.

And for Mahistruba – a wealth of treasure was awarded him for all he had done. He remembered his wife and daughter.

'If I might ask for something else, or even instead of the gold – ?'

'You shall have what you want plus the gold,' said the King.

'If I could have the ship, I'd like that. You see, I'm a sailing man and it's in a ship that I feel I become myself.'

His wish was granted. Soon they sailed in that same ship, westwards, to their homeland, watching the sunny town disappear. And whenever Mahistruba sailed the seas, from that day forward, he couldn't help but open the chest in the corner of his cabin, to stare at its empty space and to smile.

16

Maui and the Islands

THERE are many tales to tell of Maui. But to begin at the beginning, his mother, Taranga, thinking her baby had come before its time, wrapped him in a lock of her hair and cast him into the sea. Unknown to her, the baby still lived and the sea creatures adopted and nourished him until he gained fair health. He was brought to the shore again, encased inside a jellyfish, and it was here that one of his ancestors, a magician, found the little child. Immediately he took him to his home and hung him upside down on the rafters until he heard him cough and scream with life. It could be said that the sea was Maui's foster mother.

During the years that passed as Maui became a boy, he heard from his ancestor a host of wondrous tales, but more than this, he learned the art of magic. Because of his unusual childhood, and possessed with special powers, Maui was able to view life with great optimism. In fact, he was almost too carefree. There was nothing he loved more than to play a good joke.

He found his rightful family again. At his anointing ceremony, his father forgot one particular ritual and, because of this, Maui never became completely immortal. There was much of the trickster boy about him all his life.

116

It happened that his brothers did not like Maui.

'Oh, he is so idle,' they would say. 'The only things he bothers with are pranks and schemes.'

Maui's wife and children also often complained about him. The days were very long since the time when Maui had flown to the sky and held back the fast journey of the sun. Now it moved slowly, giving light enough for many hours of work in a day.

'Why not go fishing with your brothers?' asked Maui's wife. 'See, they are preparing their lines; their boat is almost ready.'

'Because,' said Maui, 'any fish I caught would be so big that before the entire village could eat it, it would be spoilt.'

'But you must do something,' said his wife, knowing that she could work better herself when he was out of the house. He watched his brothers as they strengthened the lashings that held the outrigger of their canoe. It might be a good day for some sport, he thought. So he jumped inside the canoe.

'No, no, we don't want you with us. You'll do something stupid. You'll play your tricks,' they said nervously.

Maui eyed the size of the canoe. Very big. Just what he needed. He could hide. He could turn himself into a bird or grow so tiny they'd never see him beneath the planks on the canoe-floor.

The brothers pushed their boat out to sea.

'Let's be thankful he never came,' they said, as the canoe passed beyond the reef and they began to bail water. Then they heard a peal of laughter and in an instant, there before them sat Maui.

'We must go back,' they said in alarm. 'It's no good having him with us. We must stop the canoe and return. There will be more fish on other days.'

Maui stood up. By means of his magic power, he caused the sea-shore to retreat far, far away.

'Now look what he's done. What will he do next?' they

asked each other concernedly, as they strained their eyes to try to see their home.

'Nothing. I shall do nothing,' Maui announced. 'But you should go further out to sea.'

'Further than this?' they asked, incredulous.

'Certainly. The deeper the water, the bigger the fish. I shall bail for you.'

A little afraid to disagree with him, the brothers did as he suggested, though they claimed that, out of their usual fishing grounds, their lines would not fall deep enough.

After some time, and contrary to what they had expected, the brothers drew in a massive haul of fish. Then they couldn't help thanking Maui for his magic powers and the help he had given them.

'Will you let me fish now?' he asked.

They stared at each other, unsure of what to say.

'We have enough. Let us go back,' one said.

'I have brought you this fortune. I have bailed for you and now you do not let me try for myself.'

'It's not that,' said another brother. 'It's because – um – you have no hook.'

'I have got a hook,' announced Maui and he took from his belt a piece of bone. They eyed it suspiciously.

'This hook is the jawbone of Muri, our grandmother. When I visited the underworld she knew me and she gave it to me. It has worked much magic before. With this I beat and held back the sun. Who knows what it might do today?'

The brothers were still not happy.

'And bait – you have no bait – '

At that he picked from the floor of the canoe a twist of rope. In one strong swipe, he lashed his face and his nose bled profusely. When the blood had begun to dry he smeared it over the magic jawbone.

'I have both hook and bait,' he said.

Then he peered into the depths of the sea about them and began to chant; a strange, hollow call.

118

Not long afterwards, the brothers watched Maui strain and pull until it seemed he would topple over upon them.

'He's caught something!' they cried.

Then they heard him murmur another sound; words they did not understand.

'Why, oh why, Tonga-Nui? Why do you hold so fast, so obstinate there below me?'

The brothers became fearful. They heaved together on the line. And then, to their enormous dismay, what seemed like a beast of unimaginable dimensions began to surface from the water. In their terror, they let go of their lines and fell back; Maui held fast with all his might as the sea swirled and foamed about them.

'It's true what they say,' cried one, 'that what Maui holds in his hand he cannot throw away.'

They looked to see a giant fish, the size of an island, being drawn up strongly by Maui.

'Let go! Let us leave and return to our home!' they cried.

Unknown to them, the jawbone fish-hook had hitched itself to the lintel of the house of Tonga-Nui, the grandson of Tangaroa, Lord of the Sea. Pulling as he did, Maui had managed to bring the house and the land upon which it stood to the brink of the ocean world. This fish, for fish it was, was soon seen to be dotted with palms in which lived exquisite coloured birds. Small bays contained tiny villages from whence pale coils of smoke blew and rose to disappear into the fragrant, soft air.

'I must go,' said Maui as their canoe grounded and stayed firm on this rocky fish-shore. 'I must find Tangaroa and ask his forgiveness for hauling up this land. Wait here. Do not touch or eat this precious fish. When I return we can cook the catch you won earlier. Then we'll go; we'll leave behind some food as an offering.'

With these instructions Maui left his brothers. He found a spot not far from where the canoe lay stranded and there he dug, with a shell, a small pit into which he drove the evil spirits of himself and his brothers, hoping that this gesture would placate the Lord of the Sea and his descendants.

But the brothers, entranced as they were with the rare beauty of this fish, this island that Maui had so miraculously discovered, began to want possession of it.

'One island and four of us. How shall we divide it?' they asked themselves.

No agreement between them could be found. They began to quarrel. They leapt from the boat and struck the fish, cutting and dashing its surface so that it wriggled and squirmed beneath their blows. In their anger, and being hungry after their ordeal, they sliced great pieces from it and ate them with unnatural greed. Eventually, writhing beneath their harsh treatment, the back of the fish was thrown into ridges and wrinkles.

'How it struggles!' they cried. The more they fought, the more the island fish leapt and sprang and coiled, until at last its gentle form was twisted and misshaped into mountain peaks and deep ravines. Had the brothers obeyed Maui, the island would have remained perfectly flat.

From that time on, it was known as Te Ika-a-Maui; the Fish of Maui. Its particular features bear witness to the struggle that ensued there. And other islands emerged; they rose from the ends of the lines that the brothers, in their alarm, had abandoned to the sea when they saw that first, great fish. To one end of Te Ika-a-Maui you can see a cape shaped like the jawbone fish-hook.

It was as if Maui knew the islands were there, that he had an added sense, an awareness of what lay beneath the sea. He was never a god, but his trickster deeds, often played for sheer fun, landed him always with some extraordinary adventure, thanks to his magic powers. And the islands off the coast of New Zealand may remind us of the time when Maui, escaping boredom, delighted in teasing his brothers.

17

The Enchanted Fisherman

IN the village of Panton, the men used to sit and drink together in the John O' Gaunt Inn. This was long ago, before the Bay of Morecambe could boast its fine resorts and terraced esplanades. Long ago, when the mists of the sea rose to meet the inland hills. There, from the shore, you could see the mountains tower, stark and broad, sheltering the lakes that lay within their range. The bleak, bare outlines would grow pale and dim as the night-time fog ascended.

The men, mostly fishermen, would often recount their experiences; things that had happened to them as they went about their work. Being alone in a boat gave rise to all sorts of thoughts, and from the bay, looking back at the steeply rising hills, it would not have been hard for some to allow their imaginations to run away with them. The warmth and congeniality of the fireside at the Inn also prompted their tongues to ramble on, drink after drink, night after night. Tom Grisdale swore he was often completely lost though never really far from home.

It was when Roger (so often silent as he sat at the end of the dark, oak table) began to mumble over his tankard, that the others paused and looked up.

'Bells there were. Bells that seemed to come up from the water . . . .'

'What's that you say there, Roger?'

'It was a calm night with no mist to speak of. I was out in the boat, about to leave. I'd had a fair catch and it was getting late. Then I heard them. Bells. I looked round and saw the fog had come, sudden. I was a bit afeared of it, rising up like that. But these bells; they were somewhere far off and yet near, right there. I looked round and could see nothing but white sheets of fog, swirling about me. I bent over, looking into the water. I stared right down. The sound was from there, below me. When I sat up straight again the white mist had gone. I don't know how long it was. I did know that everything was changed. The shore looked different and there was clear moonshine all over distant fells.

'I was about to hoist up sail, get on home again, but the boat started to move, all on its own. There was nothing to do. I could only sit back and see what was to happen.

'Boat reached shore, but moved alongside to a little cove. I swear it was not the same place we know. And soon I was to be certain of it. Boat stopped, up on the sand. Then I saw them; tiny folk dressed in green. They came running up towards me. They jumped and they flew – I'm not sure which; I cannot tell. They climbed into the boat and they sang these very words:

> "To the land of Ever Day
> Where all things own the Fay Queen's powers,
> Mortal come away!"

'I followed them. I couldn't help it. They took me away to a grassy spot. I could see it all in the moonshine. And there they danced in circles. I just had to stand and watch. One of them, a tiny thing, came before me and bowed. It took hold of my hand as they all moved, singing and dancing in circles. I went on; I had to go on. We came to a wood and a clearing where the moon didn't reach so well. The green folk walked now, in single file. It was very hushed. They took me to the entrance of what seemed to be a cavern; I couldn't be sure in that dim light. I knew there were steps beneath my feet, but I could not hear our tread. All I could do was hold fast to the one green creature at my hand.'

The men in the John O' Gaunt stared at one another. Some coughed, pretending the pipe smoke had got to their lungs. Others laughed openly.

'Eh Roger – we've not heard you talk this way before. You're sure your wits are with you?'

'I am sure.'

'There's no such place in this bay. Neither sandy cove nor green folk nor caverns. Come on, lad; the beer has gone to your head.'

'Let me tell you. I'll have no more beer 'til I've finished. But what I say is true.'

'Go on then, let's have it, then we shall all go home and dream the same.'

'I arrived at a beautiful glade,' Roger went on. 'There were hundreds of them, those same little green folk, and they wore small, green caps on their heads. They gave me such a welcome! They buzzed around, dancing in the air and then, after a while, as I was watching them, I realized they danced to music, like a waltz it was. I couldn't help but join in. I found myself dancing – yes, dancing. My feet were lifted from the ground. I just seemed to go on dancing this way 'til I became so very tired. I was tired like I've never known before. I noticed there was still music coming from somewhere around; perhaps from inside those tall trees. But it was different; it was quiet and nice, sort of soothing. There were smells too, like herbs and flowers together. It must have been then that I fell asleep. A deep, deep sleep.

'I cannot say how long I slept, but I knew, the very moment I woke, almost before my eyes were open, that it was all gone. There was only the grass, the trees; no green folk nor music. And then I felt this pain in my stomach. I was that hungry. I rose to my feet and looked around. I said, "How I wish I'd something to eat," and then it was there before me; food, and plenty of it. I said aloud, since I was that amazed, I said, "What luck that this should happen. And what a place! Where can I be?"

'Then one of the little greenies appeared, sort of out of nowhere.

> *"In the land of nodding flowers*
> *Where all things own the Fay Queen's powers . . . ."*
> it said.

'I couldn't help it; it was such a dear thing. I – well – I loved it. I fell in love with it. No sooner had I felt this way than the greenie turned into the most beauteous woman I ever set eyes on. She looked at me and she asked me:

"Do you bow to my power?"

'I was already in her power. I answered her with words that were true, as true as all that happened. I said:

' "I now forget my whole life up 'til this moment. I don't know where I am; I don't care. I only hope to have your face before me."

'Then she laughed. She said, "Ah, the King will not like that," and she ran away; she disappeared.

'I was left alone, more alone than ever, having met her, spoken to her and been deserted by her. I was hungry still. I wished for food and it came. I couldn't help but think how grand it would be to get money so easily. And there it was, lying on the grass before me, real gold coins.

'I thought it was time to go. There was nothing there but silence and I had this sorry feeling in my heart. The boat; I had to find it. I may as well try one way as much as another, I thought. So I moved straight ahead, through the trees.

'After some while I came to another clearing, more open than the one before, with sloping banks and tree-stumps and woodland animals hopping here and there. There were these creatures again, not the greenies, more delicate, softer. They were stitching the wings of moths and butterflies onto a fine, loose cloak that stretched to the pale shoulders of that beauty I had seen. She was sitting there, a little raised upon a moss-covered bank. She had an attendant; he seemed like a dwarf, but his dark suit was made of hard, black, beetle wings. And next to her was a man clothed in a coat of acorn cups and nutshells. They looked at each other – all the time. They never stopped their looking. Not even to see me arrive. I saw they both wore crowns.

'Something in me rose with anger; something that felt like hate for that man. I didn't like to see the way she watched him. I felt enraged and moved towards him, but when I reached the mossy bank, I fell to her feet and kissed them.

'The next thing I knew, I was being battered on the head. The blows seemed to come from all around and I saw them, those greenies, and I tried to catch hold of them. It was no use. I lay there quite confused.

' "Oh I wish I were back in my boat on the bay," I said, as I felt my head bang with pain. And when the throbbing ceased, I looked up and there I was, aboard my little skiff, stranded high on Panton beach. I blinked a deal; I thought I must have dreamed it. When I looked in my shoes and my clothes, I found no gold coins nor nothing. It was as if it had never happened.'

Roger stared into his tankard. The men at his table yawned and looked at the clock.

'Well, it's time we were all getting home,' one said, as they fingered the smoke from their pipes and moved along the bench.

They were glad to have heard Roger's tale; it passed a pleasant evening. Of course, none of them believed it at the time. But about a year later, when they saw his place at the Inn had been empty several nights, they began to search the neighbourhood. There had been a strong gale and some believed he might have been lost at sea.

Then one night, as they sat again in the John O' Gaunt, they remembered his strange tale.

They ran together, to Panton beach, and high up on the sand they found his boat upturned. With all the strength they could muster between them, they rolled it right side up. But Roger was not there.

18

Isaac and the
Parson of Brönö

ISAAC, a fisherman from Helgeland, was once out catching halibut when he felt something heavy, tugging at his line. He pulled hard and was a little dashed to find there nothing but an old sea-boot and not a halibut at all. He remained staring at it a long time until it dawned on him that this was the very boot that had once belonged to his brother. A great storm, the winter before, had taken the lives of many, his brother included. It saddened him to remember the occasion, and he was about to cast the boot back into the water when he fancied there was still something inside it. He turned quite cold at the thought.

'Now what shall I do?' he asked himself. 'I cannot take it home for it will terrify my mother. Yet back into the sea it must not go. If there is a foot there, even some toes, they ought to have some kind of burial, as is right for every human soul.'

He therefore made up his mind to see the parson of Brönö. Carrying the sopping, heavy boot at arm's length, he soon arrived at the parson's front door.

'I will not bury an old sea-boot,' said the parson emphatically.

Isaac scratched his head. He understood the parson's point, but he was anxious to do his dead brother a favour.

'Then how much of a human body do you need for him to have a decent, Christian burial?' he asked.

'I cannot tell you exactly how much of the body is required, but to be sure, a tooth or a finger or a lock of hair just will not do. How can I read the service over such things? There ought to be enough for one to see that a soul has been there. Really, a toe or two in an old sea-boot! Whatever will you think of next?'

Disappointed and still not satisfied, Isaac crept into the churchyard late at night and there he dug a hole at a respectable distance from the other graves where he buried his brother's sea-boot.

He went home feeling relieved. It was the least he could do, wasn't it, he told himself, and so much better to have that small part (however much of the foot there was) near to God's own house than abandoned in the sea.

Towards autumn he was out near the skerries in his boat again, this time on the look-out for seals. They would dive then bob to the surface, their round, shining heads appearing as if out of nowhere. When the ebb-tide left behind it tangled knots of seaweed and odd pieces of driftwood, so he saw amongst them a knife-belt with an empty sheath attached. He scooped it up with his oar and recognized it immediately as being his brother's. Examining it closer he saw how the sea had bleached the leather. He fingered the belt, remembering how together they had argued on its quality, the day they had both got very drunk. It didn't seem so long ago and how he missed him!

Throughout the long winter Isaac couldn't help hearing in his mind the words of the parson of Brönö. At the same time he wondered what he should do if ever he chanced to come across some new memento of his poor, drowned brother:

'Imagine if it were some other part of the body that a squid or a fish or even a Greenland shark had bitten off?'

When he pushed his boat out, facing those same, wild skerries where first he had found the sea-boot, he began to tremble with fear.

Then, as if to defy his own nervousness, he found he could not resist deliberately searching the area, almost in the hope that he would find something. Perhaps if his sad treasure were obviously the relics of a lost soul, the parson of Brönö might deign to give them their rightful burial.

Poor Isaac became quite distracted. He began to talk to himself. But worse than this were the dreams he had. One night, as he lay fitful and anxious in his bed, the door flew open, letting in an icy sea-blast. Isaac shivered with fear. He believed he could see his brother limping about the room, dragging one leg behind him. He thought he heard him cry and yell, begging for his foot, complaining bitterly that the sharks pulled and played with all that was left of him.

The next morning, feeling better in the light of the day, Isaac questioned himself again:

'I should not have kept it here, by itself in a lonely churchyard. And yet, why am I troubled so? It cannot be cast to the withering seas either.'

He felt he would go out of his mind with worry:

'Perhaps my poor, lost brother is in hell. Perhaps I share his torment. If only that parson would set my mind at rest.'

At last he decided he should do all he could to find enough lost material to satisfy the parson's need for evidence. He took with him all his dredging gear when next he set out for the skerries. And all he found were scraps of metal, still more seaweed and the odd starfish. It seemed Isaac would never know peace.

He was out near the rocks fishing one evening. He cast his line into the water when a hook caught one of his eyes and down, down to the bottom of the sea went that eye.

'Well, there's no use me dredging the place now,' he said. 'At least I can see enough to get home.'

During the night he lay awake with a bandage over the empty socket, tossing and writhing in pain. And as he rolled about, so he became more anxious. Things could never be so

130

black again. As soon as he had come to that decision, a most peculiar thing happened.

It was as if he was looking around him, down in the depths of the sea. There were fish lurching and snapping at an old sea-wreck, near to a line. They bit at the bait then they wriggled and escaped; all sorts of different fish. A haddock approached and remained still, mouthing the water, uncertain.

Then Isaac could hardly believe what he thought he saw. It looked like the back of a man wearing leather clothes, but one sleeve was caught between the planks of the wreck. He was trying to free himself, but to no avail.

A heavy, white halibut appeared, hovering, staring at him. It seemed to be pleading. Suddenly everything went dark. Then a voice, unspoken, more like a thought, began to sound in his ears:

'Search only in the evening, when the tide in the sound is on the ebb. And when you pull up tomorrow, let the halibut slip off the line for the hook hurts me so; it's caught on my mouth.'

The next day, trembling in anticipation, yet determined to go ahead, Isaac stole into the churchyard and chipped a piece of stone from a tomb.

'It's from God's sacred place and it might help to dredge the bottom of the sea.'

Then he waited till the evening and, when the tide had turned, went out and began his search.

When he reached a certain patch of water, the pain in his empty eye-socket began again to disturb him. He thrust down his line and immediately he felt a tug. Something, from somewhere, told him it was that great, white halibut he had seen in his dreams. He waited and the tugging disappeared. But soon another sensation of pulling, a different one, caught his attention. He drew up a broken piece of wood and clinging to this was a portion of a leather jacket. It was the arm; he knew it was the arm because he saw some fingers that straggled there, beneath the cuff.

131

He was relieved rather than alarmed by what he had found. He took it straight away to the parson of Brönö.

'What?' said the parson. 'Read the service over a washed up piece of old leather?'

'I'll throw in that old sea-boot and a knife-belt for good measure,' pleaded Isaac.

'You are impertinent. Salvage, waifs, strays and other such discarded sorts of whatnot should be advertised in the church porch.'

Isaac took a hold of himself and faced the parson squarely, staring into his eyes.

'I have almost lost my reasoning, my wits and my sanity with worry. On my conscience is that old sea-boot and now the jacket too and the things they both contain. I fear my brother is in hell and he seeks me out to save him. I must have peace of mind. Is it not your duty to calm a man's anxiety?'

'I will not waste consecrated earth on such tatters and rags as you bring me,' came the reply, as the parson closed his door.

Isaac's torment continued. At night the dreams haunted him and he fancied he saw again that same white halibut. One time it circled round and round, slowly, sadly. It was as if it were swimming in a wide net, anxious to be free. When he was out among the skerries, he felt he heard a gasping and a moaning from deep below, where the sea-boot and the jacket once had been.

People began to be afraid of Isaac.

'He seems to know exactly where the fish lie thickest, or where there's none but the odd one.'

'Second sight it is. And most strange.'

'Stranger still is what he says. "If I don't know, why, my brother does." That's what he says at times.'

The parson of Brönö heard none of this, of course. Rarely did he leave his house. But there came a time when he was required on a serious errand, out along the coast. He chose the men to take him there and one of these was Isaac. They did not take long, being used to the route close to the shore. But by the time the evening and the hour to return came round, the sea had whipped up considerably.

'Bit rough indeed,' said the parson, 'but you men know what your jobs are. Besides, I have to be back for a good night's sleep.'

They had not gone far when the gales rose and a whistling shot through the air. The rollers grew and burst in dazzling, white foam. Through the crashing waters they sailed until the pitch-black dark surrounded them. Yet still they could see the spray.

Then they crashed a rock, leaving a gaping hole in the boat's lower side. The parson of Brönö and the crew raced for the ladder to the upper deck.

'Help! Help! We are going to drown. We shall die here out at sea abandoned and forgotten. Help!' cried the parson.

Isaac remained sitting where he was, at the tiller. 'No, she won't founder,' he said quietly, though no one could hear. He was smiling to himself. He looked out to the sea; they were near the skerries. As the moon peeped from behind a wind-tossed cloud, all those aboard, the parson of Brönö, the crew and Isaac included, saw that another man was with them. He was baling out the water as fast as it poured in.

'Who's that fellow there?' called the parson, pointing his finger at the stranger. 'I don't remember hiring him. And he's baling with a sea-boot. What good'll that do to save us? Why, he's got neither breeches nor skin upon his legs. What kind of a soul is that? And the rest of him – it seems there's no more than an empty, battered old jacket . . . .'

Isaac watched the parson's alarm.

'I think you have seen him before,' he said.

The parson of Brönö grew angry:

'I demand that he leaves this boat immediately. I demand it by virtue of my sacred profession.'

'And what of the hole in our boat and the water that flows in? Will your special office save our souls? Shall we drown at sea without redemption?'

The parson was silent; he tried to think while holding on for dear life to the rail on the upper deck.

'Well,' he stammered, 'I suppose he is extremely strong despite his shabby looks. Yes, we could do with him. But there must be something he'll want in return.'

The stranger dropped the sea-boot to his frail side. He tossed back his head, turned and stared at the parson of Brönö. Then Isaac leapt to his feet and shouted up.

'Yes, there is. Only two or three shovels of earth on a rotten sea-boot and a mouldy skin jacket; that's all!'

'Very well, very well, I suppose he can enter heaven now though this gadding about has been nothing but a nuisance to me. All right. He shall have his shovelfuls of earth and his ceremony.'

Once the parson had said this, the water out among the skerries became smooth. The breakers descended into a gentle swell. The clouds dispersed.

And from that moment on Isaac knew neither daytime nor night-time troubled dreams.

19

The Seal Maiden

A FISHERMAN was walking by the shore one evening when he saw, to his great delight, a group of seal people sporting in the waves.

Now these seal people are many in number but it's not often you have the chance to see them. They live under the sea for most of the time and when they come to land they shed their sealskins and become, to all appearances, like human beings. Very soon, preferably before a new sun rises, they must return to their rightful home.

The fisherman crept behind a rock, to shield himself from their view. There he remained, watching. They leapt and they danced and laughed together, splashing in the foam with joy. Soon, they began to hurry about, taking up their sealskins to clothe themselves ready for their return.

Still fascinated by all he saw, the fisherman felt a curious urge to see what would happen if he hid one of the sealskins. He stealthily crept from the rock, his knees and back bent low, and snatched the nearest skin, returning to his hiding-place at once.

The seals splashed and barked across the tide without turning to see if all their company was present. And there, distressed and weeping, one solitary figure remained

searching the sands in haste, begging the others to wait.

'Is this what you're looking for?' called the fisherman, as he stood and held the sealskin at arms' length. But his laughter lessened as he saw the fear and horror in the deep, dark eyes before him.

She was a most lovely young woman. He saw, as she shuddered, how her black hair shone like jet. Trembling, she held up her pale, slender arms.

'Oh give me my sealskin. Without it I cannot return to my home,' she wept.

The fisherman did not listen. He could only stare at her in wonder.

'I beg of you, before the sun rises, give me back my sealskin,' she cried, and she tried to take it from him.

He grasped her arm. 'No. You are even lovelier with the dawn. You must stay with me for ever.'

She pleaded and moaned and she looked back across the sea, now glowing in the morning light. She followed the fisherman back to his home.

In time they were married. The people who came to visit often remarked on their new neighbour's exceptional beauty and asked where she had come from, but she hardly spoke a word in reply. Though he loved her and cared for her, giving her all that she might need to make her happy, the fisherman's attention was continually ignored, and he received only cold looks and weary sighs of displeasure.

In the evenings, the seal maiden vanished from the house. As he stood at his window watching her run to the sea, the fisherman's heart ached with sadness. Sometimes he followed and crept behind that same rock where he had first set eyes on her. He saw her greet the seal people and he saw the joy in her pale face as she danced and talked and waved. And always, one particular seal lingered the longest, until the first rays of a new day were just about to break across the water.

'She must never find her sealskin,' the fisherman said in sorrow and each day he checked on its hiding-place, hoping that soon she would stop her search for it and grow to love him willingly.

Five children were born to the fisherman and seal maiden. The people came and went with gifts and words of praise.

'Such lovelies,' they declared. 'And all so dark and pretty; just like their mother.'

They didn't see that between the fingers and toes of each child were small pieces of skin; the webs of sea creatures. When the children played and the seal maiden taught them all their games, she told them why they were different.

'You are my dearest friends, my darling ones. When I see your little hands and feet I know you are part of me; I remember my true home. Search, search. Search each day and never stop your searching. A black sealskin that is hidden somewhere. A skin that means much to your mother, that will make her very pleased if you should find it.'

One evening, as he sat at the table after his day's work, the fisherman noticed an unusual gleam in the seal maiden's eyes. She ladled their soup and she stacked their plates with almost an air of cheerfulness.

'At last she has grown to love me,' the fisherman said to himself.

The children seemed to share her private pleasure. They were grinning; one was positively red in the cheeks.

After their meal he heard her say good-night to each child in turn. Her voice was low and gentle; he knew she held them near and kissed them. He watched her tidy and clear each room with care and close attention. Later, when she said she could not sleep and needed to walk outside, he smiled. His heart leapt at her mildness and the warm tones of her voice.

The door slammed behind her as she left the house. He stood and watched her from the window. He saw she was racing over the fields towards the sea and in her hand was something dark and smooth; it was the sealskin. The children appeared at his side in an instant, sensing she had gone.

'Where did she find it? How – ' the fisherman exclaimed.

One child spluttered; the others stood round him.

'Tell me!'

'I – I found it, in the cornfield where we were playing. I found it underneath the haystack. I gave it to her. I knew she wanted it.'

Without waiting to hear more, the fisherman sped from the house. He raced across the fields to the clifftop and down the path to the beach. He saw the seals bounding over the waves. As he reached the water's edge he saw his own seal maiden, pulling the skin across her shoulders. With her, helping her, was that other seal, the one who had always stayed till last whenever she came to meet them.

He called out to her:

'Come back! Come back! I beg of you.'

She paused and looked at him and for a moment the fisherman thought she would return.

'You were very kind to me, I know,' she cried across the water. 'And I loved my children well.'

'Then come back,' he called, as he saw her dive forward, the sun's rays touching the tip of the foam.

'I cannot,' he heard her say. 'For I always loved my first husband better.'

20

The Boy of the
Red Twilight Sky

ON the shores of the Great Water, far out in the west, there is little to view but endless sea and the high, arching sky. There was a time when all seemed flat and colourless and the ceaseless moaning of the waves only added to the world's great gloom. The sky held no rose, no blue; it reflected the sad greyness of the sea and shore. To live there could be very lonely. One young wife, left to herself all day while her husband fished in the ocean, found her isolation almost unbearable.

'If only I had children I should not feel so bad,' she said. 'I could talk and I could busy myself with all sorts of occupations that caring for a child would bring me.'

One evening, she saw a lively kingfisher swoop and dive for minnows not far from where she sat on the shore.

'O sea-bird with your bright blue wings and white collar; how I wish we had children like you.'

The kingfisher heard her plaintive call and replied, 'Go and look you in the sea-shells; look you in the sea-shells.'

The next night, as she stared at the dull, low clouds, she saw a white sea-gull circle in the air. She followed its course as it bobbed and nosed the waves with smaller birds, just like itself.

141

'O sea-gull; how I wish we had the company of children such as yours,' she said sadly. The gull, hearing her mournful appeal replied,

'Go and look you in the sea shells; look you in the sea shells.'

She couldn't help but wonder what this twice-told advice might lead to and as she rose to make her search, she heard a strange cry from the sand-dunes behind her. Weaving her way through the spiky grasses and treading the cool, soft sand that streamed between her toes, she soon came across a large, pink shell. To her amazement and deep concern she found inside it a tiny boy. He was crying inconsolably. Without thinking how he came to be there, she lifted him in her arms and cradled him until his murmurings ceased. She then hurried home with him, anxious to await her husband and show him what she'd found. Since they both wanted children so much, they agreed that this boy should stay and live with them as their son.

They were all three very happy. His mother chatted and laughed and played with the boy. He accompanied his father on fishing trips. He helped them both in their small home, sharing with them all their household duties. He was practical and often made good use of household objects, transforming them to serve other needs. Armed with a new bow, he was able to go out hunting alone and their admiration grew when he returned from his chase with food such as they had never known before.

As he grew older he naturally changed in appearance. But instead of taking on a freckled or ruddy look as you would expect from such a hard, outdoor life, his face became refined and soft. In time it was quite golden. The warmth of his skin shone outwards so that it seemed he was surrounded by a deep, rich glow. Wherever he went he left a brilliant haze as one might trail a shadow on all sides.

'Why do you shine so brightly?' asked his mother.

'I cannot tell you yet.'

One day, a loud storm raged over the Great Water. To try to fish was impossible in such weather and the family feared they would go hungry. The torrents of wind and rain hemmed them to their house.

'Don't be afraid,' said the boy, 'for I can calm the Storm Spirit. Come with me and I will show you.'

His unwilling father unbolted the door and stood tremulous, unsure if this was wise. But the boy took his hand and led him to their boat that was moored by the dunes on the shore. They put out to sea in the howling gale and the boy looked up at the sky.

'See! See! The mad Storm Spirit is keen to overthrow us!'

The Spirit heaved and blew and tried to upset their boat, but the boy stood firm and soon the sea around them dropped and remained still. Angered by his defeat, the Storm Spirit called to the south west.

'O nephew Black Cloud – come and do your darkest work!'

Almost immediately they saw a deep shade hurtling across the sky towards them. The boy's father cried aloud in fear.

'Don't be afraid; watch,' said the boy.

As soon as he had reached the boat, Black Cloud saw the gleaming boy and felt his rays pierce through him utterly. He hurried away with speed.

At this the Storm Spirit rolled in the air with fury. Then he roared to the corners of the earth:

'O Mist of the Sea, come spread yourself and shield their view of the land.'

The boy's father crouched in the boat and moaned:

'This is the worst of all. This is the greatest enemy of fishermen. He obscures our sight and leads us to confusion.'

'Don't be afraid; watch,' said the boy.

As a pale light streamed around them, the boy sat down and smiled. Beams of gold spread out from his face and pushed the Mist of the Sea back to where it had come from. And with that, the Storm Spirit also left, screaming with rage into the distant sky.

'How have you done this?' asked the boy's father.

'When I am with you, they cannot harm you. Soon I shall tell you why.'

Remembering their present needs, they set out for the nearest fishing grounds. There the boy taught his father a magic song and as he sang it he was astonished to see, below in the water, large shoals of fish gliding into his net.

'What is the secret of your power, my son? You can lure the fish and banish the darkest weather threats.'

'Tomorrow I will tell you.'

Standing on the shore with his mother and father beside him, the following morning the boy tried his skill at shooting birds. One by one his targets fell to the earth. He tenderly skinned each bird and dried their skins with the utmost care. Across the bare sands lay all colours of feathers.

The boy, discarding his normal clothing, then dressed himself as a plover. And soon, as he waved his arms and looked across the water, he flew up into the sky. He reeled and swooped and the sea below him turned grey-white like the colour of his wings.

He descended to the shore and this time covered his body with the bright feathers of the blue jay. Up into the sky he went and the sea turned as blue as his plumage.

A third time he changed; the bright tones of the robin now covered him from head to toe and when he circled the air, the sky and the sea gleamed deepest red.

He returned to the shore once more and addressed his parents.

'My powers were tried yesterday; today they have been proved. It is time for me to leave you and return to my true home; for I am the sun's offspring. But don't think that you will not see me again. When you stand on the shore, find something white; an offering that I may see from my home in the west. For I shall be waiting and looking out for you. And you need not feel lonely. Whenever you have need of me I shall appear in the twilight sky and the sea shall reflect my glory.'

As a parting gift, the boy gave his mother a wonderful robe

144

that contained part of his power. Wearing it loosely, she could summon the Storm Spirit, Black Cloud or the Mist of the Sea. But when she sat on the sea-shore, she preferred to wrap it close about her as she watched, as she waited.

Sometimes, in the late autumn, when the evenings were chill and a greyness spread from the sky, the father and mother of the boy stood together by the sea. They threw into the air tiny white feathers and shells. They called towards the sky:

'It is dreary and dull on the shore tonight and the earth yearns for a sight of your face!'

As they watched, they saw the clouds part. The chill sea breezes touched their cheeks. Then a rose-tinged light fell from where the sky was now clear, the clouds having dispersed. It shone into their eyes and they blinked. They then looked out upon the Great Water and saw it streaked with colour; the golden glow they remembered in their son and the crimson-dappled waves of evening.

About the Stories

The Kobold and the Pirate

Legends of the Seven Seas by M. Price
(Harper & Bros., New York and London, 1929)
Kobolds are normally attached to households where, in return for their protective services, they receive great respect. Here the homeless cabin boy is guarded by a sea-faring kobold who is identified with the legendary sea-spirit, Klabauterman.

The Cormorants of Andvaer

Weird Tales from Northern Seas by R. Nisbet Bain
(Kegan Paul & Co., 1893)

The Guardian Cock

Scenes and Legends of North Scotland by H. Miller
(A. & C. Black, Edinburgh, 1860)
I have changed certain points in this legend, the events of which were said to have taken place in the time of Charles I. Originally there was no mention of the captain being cowardly, but I felt this characterization explained his actions and the supportive nature of the guardian cock. Originally, too, the captain bought the cock, but I have left the cottage uninhabited, believing its owners would not have parted with it.

Why the Sea is Salt

The Blue Fairy Book by Andrew Lang
(Longman and Co., London, 1909)
Folk Stories and Fables by E. Tappan
(Cassell & Co., London, 1909)
Although this well-known Scandinavian story takes place mainly inland, it eventually answers a question 'why' in relation to the sea. Many folktales explain, imaginatively, the nature of the world in which we live.

The Black Dragon of the Sea of Dunting

Legends of the Seven Seas by M. Price
  (Harper & Bros., New York and London, 1929)
The sea has always held an extraordinary fascination even for those who depend on it for their livelihood. Here the simple fisherman is bewildered by the unbelieving academics of the Imperial Court who cannot share his sense of wonder.

The Seal Fisher and the Roane

The Personnel of Fairyland by K. M. Briggs
  (Alden Press, Oxford, 1953)
The Fairy Mythology by T. Keightley (London, 1850)
Scottish Fairy and Folktales by G. Douglas
  (W. Scott, London, 1898).
The fisherman, in so many folktales and legends, is depicted as vulnerable, easily impressionable, fundamentally good. These are often tales that show the testing of moral judgement, and the fisherman is a perfect character to use in stories of this kind, since his work gives him easy access to the two different worlds of sea and shore and all that can happen there.

In this story the fisherman is introduced to sea-creatures he never imagined existed. The shores of Great Britain are full of them (see also *The Merrow and the Soul Cages* and *The Seal Maiden*).

A *roane* is defined by K. M. Briggs as a highland merman who travels through the sea in the form of a seal. His home is an air-filled, dry land beneath the sea. He needs his sealskin in order to travel to and from this land. Roanes are gentle, domestic creatures.

Taufatahi and Fakapatu

Myths and Legends of Polynesia by A. W. Reed
  (A. H. & A. W. Reed Ltd., Wellington, 1974)
Most giant stories take place on land where, because of their strength, giants are credited with the formation of certain mountainous features of landscape. Here it makes an amusing change to see a pair of giants engaged in personal jealousies and fears.

147

The Angry Merwife of Nordstrand

Northern Mythology by B. Thorpe
    (Edward Lumley, London, 1951)
At the sea-shore, where choices are made and so often the real point
of a story is revealed, characters may fear the sea or long to return to
it. This tale suggests that it might be wisest to stick to one's own
natural environment.

Urashima Taro

Captain Bluecoat's Wonder Tales From Japan by A. L. Whitehorn
    (London, 1921)
Legends of the Seven Seas by M. Price
    (Harper & Bros., New York and London, 1929)
This famous story, the first known account of which dates from the
eighth century, is for me typical of the nostalgic nature of many
Japanese tales. Lost time and the inability to recapture it is a
common theme in fairy tales.

Why the Sea Moans

Fairy Tales From Brazil by E. Eells
    (Dodd, Mead & Co., 1917)
A story to answer the question 'why' again. The sea-serpent is a
potential friend whose loyalty, however, is too easily forgotten. (See
also *The Sea-Captain and the Serpent*.)

Pelorus Jack

Treasury of Maori Folklore by A. W. Reed
    (Wellington, Auckland, Sydney, 1963)
This legend I brought up to date because of the interesting comment
made in A. W. Reed's book; 'The famous fish, known as Pelorus
Jack, which for more than twenty-five years escorted vessels to the
entrance of French Pass and which was protected by a special Act of
Parliament, became an almost legendary figure, even in its lifetime.
It disappeared at the end of 1916 but its true legendary origin goes
back much further. . . .' Because of the significant date, I like to
think that the peace-saving dolphin willingly left a world raging
with war.

Fairest of all Others

Dictionary of British Folktales by K. M. Briggs
   (Routledge & Kegan Paul, 1970–71)
For me, this fairy tale with its several typical motifs (the childless foster parents, the abandoned baby, the transformation of a 'bad' character through the virtue of a 'good' one) is set in the ideal place, as a story of destiny, since the inevitable movement of the tides can be seen as symbolizing life governed by that force.

The Merrow and the Soul Cages

The Personnel of Fairyland by K. M. Briggs
   (Alden Press, Oxford, 1953)
Fairy Legends and Traditions of the South of Ireland
   (John Murray, London, 1828)
The unsuspecting fisherman, as in *The Seal Fisher and the Roane* and *The Seal Maiden,* meets an unfamiliar sea-creature. Coomara, like many of the non-human characters of folktale, possesses very human traits.

   K. M. Briggs defines the *merrow* as one of the Irish merpeople who, like roanes, live on dry land beneath the sea. They, however, need their red caps to enable them and their guests to pass through the water.

Duke Magnus and the Mermaid

The Fairy Mythology by T. Keightley (London, 1850).
I adapted the story from a rather unsatisfactory translation of a ballad from Småland, a note at the end of which states that 'Magnus was the youngest son of Gustavus Vasa. He died out of his mind. It is well known that insanity pervaded the Vasa family for centuries.'

The Sea Captain and the Serpent

Tales of a Basque Grandmother by F. Carpenter
   (Doubleday, Doran & Co., Garden City, N.Y., 1930).
The sea-serpent, as in *Why the Sea Moans*, offers itself as a potential friend. Here the serpent rewards the captain for his care.

Maui and the Islands

Myths and Legends of the Polynesians by J. C. Anderson
   (Charles E. Tuttle Co., 1958)
Myths and Legends of Polynesia by A. W. Reed
   (A. H. & A. W. Reed, Ltd., Wellington, 1974)
Treasury of Maori Folklore by A. W. Reed
   (A. H. & A. W. Reed, Ltd., Wellington, 1974)
Maori Myths and Tribal Legends by A. Alpers
   (John Murray, London, 1964)

Mythology, to put it very simply, grew out of questioning. How do we come to be here? Why is the world as it is? Religion may help to provide some answers now, but long before Christianity, Islam or Buddhism, we had to turn to nature (physical nature and the nature of ourselves) to work out a few answers. However, the creation of the world, throughout the world, is usually ascribed to gods and goddesses of some kind (perhaps showing our need for them).

When Sir George Grey was sent from Britain to the South Pacific where he eventually became Governor, as recently as the middle of the last century, he found the people there still believing in their old gods, despite the fact that Christianity had reached them. He felt he should record their tales in order to understand the people.

There are whole 'families' of legends in Polynesia, the Maui stories being one of them. These tales are very much to do with creation, but more specifically with *local* creations. Maui is not a universal creator, but a demigod. He is mischievous and engagingly human. His human brothers' suspicion of him is a common feature of the tales. He stole fire from his grandmother and so brought the ability to cook to the world; he slowed down the sun so people could work longer in daylight. Eventually he died wanting to conquer death.

In this story where he 'discovers' the island of Maui, there is always a little confusion as to what exactly it was that he fished up. Was it a fish (it wriggles when the brothers chop at it) or was it an island (with populated villages intact)? One has to accept the magic of the myth; that it was both things at the same time.

150

The Enchanted Fisherman

Goblin Tales of Lancashire by J. M. Bowker
 (W. Swan Sonnenschein & Co., London, 1883)
Dreamlike lands in legend or fairy tale are often accessible only via water.

Isaac and the Parson of Brönö

Weird Tales From Northern Seas by R. Nisbet Bain
 (Kegan Paul & Co., 1893)

The Seal Maiden

Scottish Fairy and Folk Tales by W. Scott (London, 1893)
The Fairy Mythology by T. Keightley (London, 1850)
and many other books.
Variants of this story turn up all over the world. The maiden here is a Scottish seal, but depending on where her story is told, I've found her as an Indian fish, a Polynesian shark and in Lapland she emerges from the sea as a nymph straight away. The story is basically the same wherever it is told and its survival, despite travel, illustrates the idea that the folktale usually contains some universal message.

The Boy of the Red Twilight Sky

Canadian Fairy Tales by Cyrus Macmillan
 (John Lane, London, 1928)
To quote the author of the above book, he explains in his preface how his stories go back to 'very early days beyond the dawn of Canadian history' and long before King Arthur's time. He collected the tales 'by river and lake and ocean where sailors and fishermen still watch the stars; in forest clearings where lumbermen yet retain some remnants of the old vanished voyageur life and where Indians still barter for their furs. . . .'